WILLIAM—THE BOLD

By the Same Author

PURPLE WITH FURY, THE GENERAL ADVANCED ON
THEM, BRANDISHING A CARROT

(See page 94)

WILLIAM—
THE BOLD

BY
RICHMAL CROMPTON

ILLUSTRATED BY
THOMAS HENRY

LONDON
GEORGE NEWNES LIMITED
TOWER HOUSE, SOUTHAMPTON STREET
LONDON, W.C. 2

First Published	.	. .	*1950*
Second Impression	.	. .	*1952*
Third Impression	.	. .	*1955*
Fourth Impression	.	. .	*1958*
Fifth (Abridged) Impression		.	*1963*

Printed in Great Britain by
Cox & Wyman Ltd., London, Fakenham and Reading

CONTENTS

CHAPTER I

VIOLET ELIZABETH WINS

"IT'S a long time since we did a play," said William, kicking a stone from one side of the road to the other.

"Well, the las' one we did wasn't much good," said Ginger, stopping the stone more by luck than skill and returning it to William together with a large part of the road's surface.

"That was 'cause you all started fightin'," said William, falling into the ditch in his efforts to stop Ginger's stone from going there.

"Well, it was about a war, wasn't it?" said Douglas, helping to pull him out. "People do fight in wars, don't they?"

"Yes, but you needn't have gone on fightin' all the time," said William, removing some of the mud from his person with a perfunctory movement of a grimy hand.

"Well, some wars do go on a long time," said Henry with a modest air of erudition. "There was one in hist'ry that went on for a hundred years an' ours only went on for about half an hour."

"Well, you fought so much there wasn't any play left," said William.

"You fought, too," Douglas reminded him.

"I was fightin' to stop you fightin'," William explained and added, after a slight pause, "well, I did sort of get int'rested in fightin', but I didn't start it. An' any-way it spoilt the play, 'cause we'd forgot what the play was about by the time we'd finished fightin'."

"It was a jolly good fight," said Ginger a little wistfully.

"It was a jolly good play, too," said William. "I wrote it, so I ought to know."

"Well, what about this new one?" said Douglas.

The four Outlaws were walking along the road towards the village. They had, as a matter of course, spent their pocket money on the day they received it, but they were going to inspect the sweet shop window with a view to planning future purchases. This process was a never failing source of interest both to the Outlaws and the shopkeeper. The shopkeeper had served as a commando during the war and he found that the Outlaws' daily visits kept him in practice and imparted a little zest to a drab peacetime existence.

"I've been sort of thinkin' about it," said William slowly. "I was thinkin' about it while ole Markie was tellin' us about opticians in arithmetic yester-day."

"Octagons," said Henry.

"Well, I said that, didn't I?" said William pug-naciously.

"No, you didn't."

"I did."

"You didn't."

"I did."

"You didn't."

A spirited wrestling match decided the point in William's favour, and they continued their progress down the road.

"1 think a hist'ry play'd be a nice change," said William.

"They fought in hist'ry," said Ginger with anticipatory relish. "They fought all the time."

"Well, you're not goin' to fight in this one," said William firmly. "There were bits of peace here an' there in hist'ry an' we're goin' to have one of them."

"Which?" said Douglas.

"Well, we could have that bit when Queen Elizabeth had finished fightin' the French an' before she started fightin' anyone else."

"What did she do when she'd finished fightin' the French?" said Ginger, looking at Henry as their usual source of information.

"She got 'Calais' carved on her chest some time or other," said Henry vaguely.

"She *couldn't* have," said Douglas. "You mus' mean tattooed."

"All right. Tattooed, then," agreed Henry.

"That'd take a bit of time," said William. "There mus' have been quite a bit of peace then."

"Can I be Queen Elithabeth, pleathe, William?" said a small shrill well-known voice behind them.

They wheeled round and stood scowling fiercely down at Violet Elizabeth Bott. She looked up at them, smiling appealingly, fluttering long lashes over forget-me-not blue eyes, exerting all her six-year-old charm. Few hearts so stony as not to be melted by the sight . . . but the Outlaws' hearts were among the few. They continued to scowl at her in resentment and disapproval.

"Who said *you* could come tagging along with us?" said William.

"No one did," said Violet Elizabeth serenely. "I juth came."

"Well, now you've come, you can kindly go away again," said William.

He spoke with more conviction than he felt. Never in the whole course of his acquaintance with Violet Elizabeth had he known her to comply with that particular request—or indeed with any other.

"Go away," said Ginger.

"An' scream if you want to," said Douglas, anticipating her plan of campaign. "We don't care."

"You can cry if you want to, too," said Henry. "We don't care about that either."

Violet Elizabeth threw them a speculative glance, and, deciding that both those particular tactics would be wasted on this particular occasion, contented herself by letting the corners of her mouth droop wistfully and heaving a deep sigh.

"All right," she said and, turning away, began to walk slowly back along the road.

This feint did not for a moment deceive the Outlaws. They were too much accustomed to it. They walked on for a few yards in a strained and unnatural silence, then Douglas threw a wary half-glance round.

"She's comin' along after us again," he said morosely. "I knew she would."

"Well, we'll jus' take no notice of her," said William. "We'll jus' carry on as if she wasn't there. She'll soon get tired of it."

Experience should have taught him the falsity of this last statement, but William was ever an optimist.

Their arrival at the sweet shop drove Violet Elizabeth's unwelcome presence from their minds, and they stood in a row, flattening their noses against the glass, surveying the tantalising feast outspread on the other side.

"Bulls' Eyes!" said William. "Those big striped ones. I bet," gloomily, "they'll be gone by nex' Sat'day."

"Go in an' ask him to keep us some," said Ginger.

"He never does," said William. "The last time I asked him, he nearly pulled my ears off."

"Lollipops!" breathed Douglas ecstatically. "They're super, those lollipops are."

"Jelly babyth are nithe, too," said the small shrill voice behind them.

With a great effort of will, they ignored it.

"Look! There's some real stick-jaw toffee," said Henry. "I had some las' month an' it was wizard."

"I onthe had a tooth pulled out by thtickjaw toffee," said Violet Elizabeth proudly. "It wath loothe an' the thtickjaw toffee got thtuck on it and it came right out. I wath very brave. I didn't cry."

Again they ignored her.

"Wonder if he'd let us have some if we promised to bring our money first thing Sat'day mornin'," said William.

"No, he won't," said Ginger. "He jumped over the counter an' only jus' missed murderin' me the las' time I asked him."

"Well, we could give him somethin' for them," said William thoughtfully. "We've never tried that. I've got lots of things I bet he'd find useful. I've got this handkerchief my aunt sent me las' Christmas." He took a dubious-looking object from his pocket. "I bet it cost more than a few ole humbugs. It's got pictures on it. At least "—inspecting it—"it has when it's clean."

"Yes, an' look!" said Ginger, suddenly becoming fired by enthusiasm for the idea, " I'll throw my garters in." He stripped off those much-enduring articles and inspected them critically. They wore a strained and battered look, as the result of their part-time occupation as catapults. "They're jolly good garters an' garters are jolly useful things. They cost a lot of money, too. My mother's always grumbling about what a lot of money she spends on 'em. I bet they're a jolly sight more valu'ble than a few ole lollipops, anyway."

"Do you think he'd give me thome jelly babyth in exchange for one of my thockth?" piped Violet Elizabeth.

"No, of course he won't," said William.

A slow complacent smile overspread Violet Elizabeth's small countenance. Sooner or later she could always goad William into a recognition of her presence.

"Let's try, anyway," said William.

Henry added a small shrivelled apple from his pocket and Douglas a Canadian stamp, then William, as delegate, entered the shop, his expression conveying a mixture of hopefulness and apprehension.

"He can only say 'no,'" said Henry with a man-of-the-world air.

"I've known him say more than that," said Douglas darkly.

Douglas's fears were justified. A bellow of rage from inside the shop was followed by William's hasty exit, accompanied by his collection of offerings. William picked himself and his collection of offerings up from the pavement and rubbed the side of his head.

"Well, it didn't come off," he said, "but"—philosophically—"it was worth tryin'."

"Saucy little 'ound!" said the shopkeeper, appearing at the shop door. "Off with you!"

"All right," said William, "and"—untruthfully—"we wouldn't eat your rotten ole sweets now—not if you *gave* them us."

With that, the Outlaws hastened their steps down the village street. The shopkeeper made a feint of pursuing them; then, cheered and invigorated by the little scene, returned to his uninspiring daily round.

"I put my tongue out at him ath far ath it would go," said Violet Elizabeth when they stopped to draw breath.

"Don't take any notice of her," William warned the others.

"Well, let's get back to this play idea," said Henry. "Who shall we be?"

"Well, who *was* there in hist'ry?" said William. "Besides Queen Elizabeth, I mean."

"I'm going to be Queen Elithabeth," said Violet Elizabeth.

"You are *not*," said William.

"There was Thomas à Becket an' Henry the Fifth an' Dick Turpin an' Friar Tuck," said Henry.

"It's goin' to be jolly difficult dressin' up as all those," said Douglas. "You've gotter have historical clothes to act historical people."

"Queen Elithabeth walked about on people'th coatth," said Violet Elizabeth. "I onth thaw a picture of her in a book and thee wath walking about on people'th coatth."

"She's thinkin' about that man Raleigh that made cigarettes," explained Henry.

"Don't take any notice of her," said William.

"*Tell* you what!" said Ginger.

"Yes?"

"Archie's got some acting clothes. He sometimes paints hist'ry pictures, you know, an' he dresses up that ole dummy thing of his in them."

"All right," said William. "Let's go an' ask him to lend us some."

Tristram Archibald Mannister, known to the whole neighbourhood as Archie, was an artist who lived in Honeysuckle Cottage at the end of the village. He belonged to the aggressively "modern" school of painting, but, when hard pressed for cash, would return to more conventional methods and paint idealised scenes from history, which appeared before the public in the form of calendars and Christmas cards. When first he came to the village his twin sister Auriole had shared the cottage with him, but Auriole had now set up an Arts and Crafts centre in the Lake District, where her disciples wove and dyed and carved and embroidered with an enthusiasm equalled only by their lack of skill, and Archie occupied the cottage alone.

There were no signs of activity about the cottage as the Outlaws and Violet Elizabeth approached it. The garden was wild and overrun, for Archie was no gardener. Through the open kitchen window could be seen the remains of what sketchy meals Archie had consumed during the last few days, for Archie was no housekeeper and his "daily woman" was away ill. Saucepans and crockery covered the table and over-flowed on to the floor. Among them a packet of salt had spilled its contents into a tin of shoe polish, while in the sink a flue-brush appeared to have made its nest in a dish of mashed potato.

Archie himself opened the door to them. Every-thing about him that could be long and thin was long and thin. His body was long and thin, his face was long and thin, his nose was long and thin. His beard was of recent cultivation and had a sheepish, slightly furtive air, but it was obviously doing its best to be long and thin. His face wore that look of startled exasperation common to the faces of those who answered William's assault upon their door knockers. The echoes of that sustained operation was only now beginning to die away.

"You needn't break the whole place down," he said. "I'm not deaf."

So accustomed was William to this greeting that he did not trouble to reply to it.

"Can we come in, Archie?" he said and, before Archie could rally his shattered forces, the four Outlaws, with Violet Elizabeth at their heels, had entered the narrow passage-way.

"No!" said Archie, then, realising that it was too late, added irritably: "What do you want?"

William knew that demands such as he had in mind must not be blurted out in the first moment of a visit. The path to them must be paved by polite if meaning-less social trivialities.

"I hope you're quite well, Archie," he said, assuming the glassy smile and slightly imbecile expression that constituted his "company manners." "We're quite well, thank you."

"I've got a bit of a cold," said Douglas, who was a stickler for accuracy.

"I had a bit of a chilblain las' week," said Henry, not to be outdone, "but it's better now."

"It wasn't much of a chilblain," said Ginger. "I saw it."

"Well, I never said it was, did I?"

At this point Violet Elizabeth found her way into the kitchen and gave a scream of delight.

"Oo, what a lovely meth!" she said. "I'm goin' to clean up."

"We'll come into your studio an' sit down a bit if you like, Archie," said William, realising that, in Archie's present mood, it devolved upon him, William, to play the parts of both host and guest.

"Well, I don't like," said Archie bluntly.

There was no doubt that Archie was not at his best. Actually Archie was at his worst. He had been planning an exhibition of his work in London, but at the last minute had had to give up the idea owing to lack of funds. His finances had, indeed, reached so low an ebb that he had reluctantly decided to abandon his "modernistic" efforts for a time and set about a picture that would look well on calendars and Christmas cards and bring in a bit of money. He had started one the day before, but couldn't get on with it.

"We don't mind jus' stayin' a minute or two," said William, tactfully ignoring his host's outburst of irritability, "but——"

At this moment a crash of crockery from the kitchen

caused a diversion, and Archie threw a harassed glance in its direction.

"It's only Violet Elizabeth cleanin' up," said William, closing the kitchen door, so as to spare Archie the painful spectacle of Violet Elizabeth sweeping cups, plates, saucers together and carrying an armful of them towards the sink. "Let's leave her in there. She can't bother us while she's in there. Well, come on in."

With a lordly gesture he ushered his band into the studio. Archie followed helplessly.

"Look here, boys," he said, "I'm very busy. I'm——"

The rest of the sentence was drowned by another crash from the kitchen. Archie's face, twisted in anguish, was again turned in its direction. He was obviously in something of a dilemma. If he went into the kitchen to put a stop to Violet Elizabeth's activities there, he would have to leave the Outlaws to their own devices in the studio, and he had had bitter experience of what the Outlaws could do when left to their own devices.

"She'll be all right," said William carelessly. "If she hurts herself she'll yell out quick enough. . . . Well," he waved an imperious hand at his followers, "go on. Sit down."

They sat down, and there was a short silence, during which Archie's hunted look went from one to another. Then William cleared his throat and returned to the social small-talk that was to pave the way to his request.

"It's a nice day, isn't it, Archie?" he said in the high-pitched unnatural voice that went with the glassy smile and imbecile expression.

"It's not very," said Douglas. "It's been rainin'."

"Well, it's cleared up, hasn't it?" said Ginger, supporting William.

"An' anyway," said William with spirit, "it's jus' one of the things you say, like 'how are you.' It doesn't axshully mean it's a nice day."

"Why did you say it was, then?" said Douglas.

"Oh, shut up," said William.

Archie turned to them with the courage of despair, but before he could give vent to his feelings William had risen from his seat and approached a painting on the easel. It represented a long white road, bordered by trees.

"What's that?" he said.

Archie looked at it, and gloom enveloped his long, thin countenance.

"It's called 'The High Road'," he said.

"What's that thing in the middle?" said William.

"It's a tramp," said Archie rather coldly.

"Doesn't look like a tramp to me," said William. "It looks more like a tree."

"Looks a bit like a horse to me," said Ginger.

"Or a pillar box," said Henry.

"Or a tent," said Douglas.

"Anyway it doesn't look like a tramp," said William, summing up their impressions.

"I know it doesn't," snapped Archie testily. "I've been trying to make it look like a tramp and I can't."

"Well, never mind what it looks like," said William. "Things do look like other things sometimes. You can't help it." Then, thinking that he had wasted enough time on preliminaries, he went on, "What we really wanted was, will you lend us some of your acting clothes for our hist'ry play?"

"My what?" said Archie, outraged.

"Your acting clothes," said William. "Those things you dress that doll thing of yours up in."

"I have a few historical costumes," said Archie frigidly, "that I use occasionally on my lay figure, but I do not lend them to children."

"Well, we're not really children," said William persuasively. "I mean, after all, we're eleven. I mean, we've got a bit of sense."

"I'm eleven and three quarters and a bit," said Henry.

"I bet we could take care of a few hist'ry clothes all right," said Ginger. "I once got eight out of ten for hist'ry. At least," with a burst of honesty, "it looked like eight."

"It turned out to be three," Douglas reminded him.

"I once had to write out the date of the battle of Waterloo a hundred times," said William, "so I ought to know a bit of hist'ry."

"What was the date of the battle of Waterloo?" Henry challenged him.

William hesitated.

"Ten sixty-six," he said at last uncertainly.

"It wasn't," said Henry.

"It was," said William, gathering certainty from opposition.

"It wasn't."

"It was."

"Will you all please go away!" said Archie desperately. "I tell you I'm busy. I don't want you here. Go—*away*!"

He advanced upon them. There was a gleam in his eye suggestive of a wild animal at bay. They retreated. Another crash from the kitchen diverted his attention for a moment—but only for a moment. The Outlaws backed before him into the narrow passage hall. And then—quite suddenly as it seemed—they found themselves outside the closed front door. The slamming of the door coincided with a clatter of falling saucepans from the kitchen and Violet Elizabeth's voice upraised lightheartedly if unmelodiously in a snatch of song.

The Outlaws walked slowly down to the gate.

"Well, *that* wasn't any good," said Douglas. "I knew it wouldn't be."

"He was in a rotten temper," said William. "I wasted a jolly lot of p'liteness on him, but it wasn't any good."

"P'raps we'd better give up this hist'ry play idea," said Ginger.

"No, we won't," said William, who never admitted the failure of his plans. "We'll wait till he's in a good temper an' then try again."

"We'll probably have to wait till we're old men," said Douglas, giving his wit the tribute of a hollow laugh.

"My aunt once went to a play," said Henry, "where a man called Hamlet acted Shakespeare in ordin'ry clothes. So it would be all right to act a hist'ry play in ordin'ry clothes. We could jus' wear a few saucepans an' things to show it was hist'ry."

"No, we won't," said William. "We'll do it in hist'ry clothes. We'll get Archie in a good temper an' borrow his hist'ry clothes."

"An' p'raps you'll kin'ly tell us how you're goin' to do

that," said Ginger with a somewhat laboured imitation of William's sarcastic manner. "P'raps you'll kin'ly tell us how you're goin' to put someone in a good temper that you've jus' been pushed out of his house by."

"Well, people *do* get back into good tempers out of bad ones," said William. "My father does sometimes. He comes in from the office in an awful temper an' then if there's chicken or somethin' for dinner he gets back into a good one."

"An' p'raps you'll kin'ly tell us," said Ginger, "how we're goin' to get Archie chicken for dinner. P'raps you'll kin'ly tell us——"

"Oh, shut up sayin' that," said William irritably. "You're always the same. You go on makin' objections an' objections. . . ." He stopped suddenly in the middle of the road, obviously struck by an idea. "*Tell* you what!"

They gathered round him expectantly. Whether practical or not, William's ideas were always worth listening to.

"Yes?"

"Well," said William slowly, "I bet he was really in a bad temper about that picture, 'cause he couldn't get that tramp right. It looked like a tree."

"A horse," said Ginger.

"A pillar box," said Henry.

"A tent," said Douglas.

"Well, we can't do anythin' about that," said Ginger.

"Yes, we can," said William.

"What can we do?"

"We can find him a model."

They considered this in silence for some moments, then:

"I'M CLEANING UP FOR YOU, ARCHIE," SAID VIOLET
ELIZABETH.

"My aunt's got a new dress that's a model," said Ginger vaguely, "but I don't s'pose she'd lend it us. She made an awful fuss jus' 'cause I dropped a bit of ice cream on it."

"Well, we don't want a dress anyway," said William. "We want a tramp. Artists 've got to have *people* for models when they're paintin' people."

"Why?" said Douglas.

"Well, so's to be sure to get their faces in the right place an' that sort of thing," said William impatiently. "I wish you'd try'n' have a bit of *sense*."

"I know a boy that's got a model motor launch," said Douglas, "an'——"

"Oh, shut up!" said William. "It's a *tramp* we want, I tell you, not a dress or a boat. Now listen. If we got Archie a tramp for a model, then he could draw it prop'ly an' get into a good temper again an' then he'd let us have his actin' clothes."

"But how can we?" said Douglas.

"There aren't any tramps now," said Henry, "'cause the government make 'em have doctors an' wear spectacles an' that stops 'em bein' tramps."

"P'raps you'll kin'ly tell me——" began Ginger and stopped abruptly, quelled by the light of battle in William's eye.

"Now listen," said William again. "We've got to go an' have a good look for a tramp. I bet they've not all got doctors an' spectacles. Anyway, we can go'n' *look*, can't we?"

"We've never had much luck with tramps," said Douglas despondently. "When we *do* find 'em, it gen'rally turns out we'd have been better off if we hadn't."

"Well, we're not goin' to get anythin' done if we stay here arguin' an' arguin' an' arguin'," said William. "I'm goin' to look for a tramp, an' if you don't want to come you needn't."

"Yes, we'll come," chorused the other three.

They began to walk on down the road.

"Where are you goin' to start lookin'?" said Ginger.

"I'm goin' to start lookin' in the woods," said William. "Most of the tramps I've found have been in woods. They go to woods so's they can sit down an' eat their dinners without bein' run over."

They scrambled over the stile and made their way across the field towards the wood. Suddenly William stopped and a slow smile overspread his face.

"We've got rid of Violet Elizabeth, anyway," he said. "We've left her in Archie's cottage."

The same thought had just struck Archie. He stood, the harassed, hunted look still on his face, outside the kitchen door; then, gathering his courage, flung it open. A scene of hideous devastation met his eyes. The floor swam in soapy water, on the surface of which floated a small fleet of broken crockery, together with half a loaf, a packet of cigarettes, some bills and circulars, a tie, a pair of braces, a tea-cosy and various kitchen implements. In the middle of all this knelt Violet Elizabeth, enveloped to the chin in the char-woman's apron, slopping blissfully about with a dish-cloth and Archie's best clothes brush. She raised a face that was streaked with dirt but radiant with joy and pride.

"I'm cleanin' up for you, Archie," she said. "I'm thcrubbing the floor."

"Oh, my gosh!" groaned Archie.

"I've wathed up thome of your thingth," said Violet Elizabeth, "but they got a bit thlippery with the thoap and thome of them got broken but I thpect they'll mend."

"Oh, Jehosophat!" moaned Archie as his eye took in further details.

"I found thome thtuff in the cupboard called 'Plate Powder'," said Violet Elizabeth, "tho I wathed your plateth with it. It made a lovely meth. I'm going to clean your windowth when I've finithed thcrubbing the floor."

"No, don't," said Archie wildly. "Please don't."

"It ithn't any trouble at all," Violet Elizabeth assured him graciously as she sluiced the water round and sent little cascades up on to his trousers. "I'm going to uthe pumith thtone to clean your windowth with."

"No, please——" wailed Archie, but at this point he was summoned to the hall by the rat-tat-tat of the postman's knock. The letter was from his eldest sister. He took it to the studio and opened it with a sense of misgiving. Archie's eldest sister disapproved of Archie. She disapproved of his beard, his colourful low-necked shirts, his Bohemian tendencies and his artistic activities. Her letters were never very pleasant reading.

DEAR ARCHIBALD [he read],

Aunt Georgina is over in England and is coming to see you to-morrow afternoon. She wants to take you by surprise, but I thought I ought to let you know. She hasn't seen you since your christening, and I've done my best to prepare her for the worst. I've warned her about your beard and the extraordinary way you dress and talk and behave. She doesn't appear to mind that, but she seems to have a sort of

superstitious feeling about the Georgian silver tea-pot
that she sent you on your twenty-first birthday.   It's
evidently a family heirloom.   If you've treasured that,
I gather that there's nothing she won't do for you—
even to financing the exhibition of your pictures in
London.   I hope that you will make a favourable
impression, but I'm afraid that I have little confidence
in your doing so.

Your affectionate sister,

EUPHEMIA.

The hunted expression on Archie's face changed to
one of nightmare panic.   The Georgian tea-pot.   He
had vague memories of a Georgian tea-pot, but he didn't
know what he'd done with it.   It must be somewhere.
He opened a tall cupboard that stood behind the door,
full to overflowing of all manner of junk, and began
to burrow in it like a terrier after a rat.   Paint pots,
paint brushes, sketching blocks, boots, shoes, cushions,
an old tennis racket, an older pair of skates, a still
older pair of household scales, books, magazines, a
barometer, a fur-lined waistcoat, flew out in a shower
around him.   Things he hadn't seen for years appeared
as if by magic.   But the tea-pot was not among them.
He bundled the things back and stood there considering. . . .   Perhaps it was in the garden shed.   He
might have used it for nails or labels, or for mixing
his tomato fertiliser in one of his short-lived spasms
of gardening enthusiasm.   Then he re-read the letter
and another thought struck him.   Aunt Georgina was
coming this afternoon.   She would be here for tea.

His mind went over his sketchy domestic arrangements.   He had some tea and he had some milk, but

he had no cake. One always gave aunts cake for tea. He would go out and buy some cake before he continued his search for the tea-pot. He went to the front door, then paused, arrested by fresh sounds from the kitchen. He opened the door. The room was full of acrid smoke. Violet Elizabeth, now sodden with water and covered with soot, was in the process of cleaning the stove both outside and in, with the help of a bucket of water and a feather duster.

"Go away, Archie," she said imperiously. "I'm buthy. I'm thpring cleaning. Ithn't it kind of me to thpring clean your houthe for you?"

Archie gulped and swallowed.

"Yes—er—thank you so much," he said, "but I have to go out and get some cake now, so I—I think you'd better go home."

"Don't be thilly," said Violet Elizabeth. "I can't go home yet. I haven't finithed. I than't have finithed for ageth and ageth."

Archie summoned what remained of his fighting spirit.

"You're making a dreadful mess," he said.

"People alwayth make a meth, thpring cleaning," said Violet Elizabeth. "Thath why they do it. Now go away and thtop being a nuithanthe, thereth a good man."

"I wish you'd——" began Archie, but Violet Elizabeth, abandoning finesse, had taken the floating half-loaf and flung it at him. It hit him full in the face, and he instinctively turned to flight, closing the kitchen door to serve as a bulwark between him and the redoubtable child. There seemed nothing left for him to do but go out and buy a cake. I expect she'll soon get tired of it and go away, he assured himself, as he wiped the half-loaf off his face with his handkerchief. . . . And at least I've cleared those boys off, he thought as he got out his bicycle and pedalled away in the direction of Hadley. I've cleared them right off and they aren't likely to come back. . . .

That, of course, was where Archie was wrong. The Outlaws were already on their way back, in company with an individual whose reddish beard, open-necked shirt of nondescript hue and bedraggled velveteen jacket struck a note that was both casual and picturesque. He walked with a jaunty swing, carrying a knotted twisted stick and a large bundle enveloped in a faded red handkerchief.

The Outlaws had found him, as William had predicted, in the wood, and he had shown, from the first, considerable interest in their proposition.

"'E'll make it worth me while, o' course," he had stipulated. "I'm in great demand fer tramp pictures. Hartists all over the world—well, they queue up fer me, as you might say. I've got a waitin' list a mile long. I'm on me way now from one famous hartist to another. Royal Arcadians, they are, both of 'em."

"Academicians," said Henry.

"Well, one of them things, anyway," said the tramp with lighthearted indifference. "There's paintings of me in hevery British Museum in hevery city throughout the world. So, much as I'd like ter do it fer nothin', I've gotter charge, an' my charges is——" He threw them a speculative glance. "'Ow much does 'e pay?"

"Well, I dunno quite," said William.

"Gardeners get about two shillings an hour," said Henry.

"Ah, yes," said the tramp, "but this 'ere modellin' wot I do's more skilled work than gardenin'. All a gardener's got to do is to shove a spade into the earth, but this 'ere modellin' takes skill. It takes skill an' imagination an' knowledge of the world same as I've got, an' you've gotter pay for them. Five shillin's an hour they're worth to any hartist. Why, I've bin offered five guineas an hour by Royal Arcadians to let 'em paint me to 'ang in the British Museum, but, o' course, I won't charge this 'ere friend o' yours that much."

"No, he couldn't afford that," said William, remembering Archie's chronic state of impecuniosity.

"Well, seein' 'e's a pal of yours, I'll do 'im cheap," said the tramp, twirling his stick jauntily through the air. "I'll do 'im dirt cheap. I'll put 'im in now in front of all this waitin' list an' I'll only charge 'im 'arf a crown an hour."

"That's jolly good of you," said William gratefully.

"Yes, I 'spect he'll pay that," said Ginger.

For Archie, though generally in sore financial straits, was notoriously lavish. He paid anyone anything they asked and seldom counted his change. If ever he did count it, he counted it wrong.

"An' he'll be so grateful to us he's bound to let us have his acting clothes now," said William.

"Well, come on," said Henry. "Let's go back quick to the cottage. . . . I say, if he's got a suit of armour I could be Henry the Fifth."

"No, you couldn't," said William. "If anyone's going to be Henry the Fifth, it's me. You can be one of his wives if you like. He had six, an' one of them haunts the Houses of Parliament."

"You're thinkin' of Guy Fawkes," said Henry.

"I am *not*," said William. "I ought to know what I'm thinkin' of, considering it's me that's thinkin' of it. Quite a lot of hist'ry's comin' back to me. I know a jolly lot more than I thought I did when I started thinkin'."

"It's a tirin' job, this 'ere modellin'," said the tramp. "I 'opes a little refreshment's thrown in, as it were. I can't give me best if I'm 'ungry an' thirsty. Thirst's the greatest torment to a modeller."

"That'll be all right," Ginger reassured him. "I know he's got some lemonade."

"Oh, 'as 'e?" said the tramp without enthusiasm.

Only Douglas seemed to feel some slight misgiving about the undertaking.

"I hope it's going to be all right," he said. "I've got a sort of feeling that something's goin' to go wrong with it."

"You always have," said William. "I've never known you do anythin' without havin' a sort of feeling that somethin's going to go wrong with it."

"Yes, an' it gen'rally does," said Douglas.

The tramp was evidently warming to the prospect of his new employment.

"If there's anythin' else he'd like me ter model for," he said, "I'll do it willin' fer a consideration. 'Igh-ups or anythin'. I can act posh as good as anyone."

They were approaching Archie's cottage now, and instinctively they slackened their pace. A faint anxiety invaded William's countenance.

"Of course," he said thoughtfully, "we'll have to

'splain about you. I 'spect, when we've 'splained about you, he'll be grateful all right. P'raps—p'raps you'd better stay at the gate while I 'splain."

The three Outlaws and their new friend stood at the gate while William performed his famous tattoo on the knocker. There was no answer. Cautiously William opened the door and went inside.

"Archie!" he called.

There was still no answer.

He opened the kitchen door. Violet Elizabeth had finished the floor and the stove. The floor still swam with water, on which floated most of Archie's domestic equipment. The stove still emitted clouds of acrid smoke. Violet Elizabeth now stood on a chair "cleaning" the window with a piece of pumice stone.

"Go away," she ordered imperiously. "I'm buthy. I'm thpring-cleaning. I don't want boyth in here."

"And we jolly well don't want to be in here," said William. "Where's Archie?"

"He'th gone out," said Violet Elizabeth, gazing with mild interest at the crack that had suddenly appeared in the window's surface, then setting to work again with renewed vigour.

"Where?"

"I don't know. He'th gone to get thome caketh an' if you don't go away, I'll thcream an'——"

But William had rejoined his friends at the gate.

"He's out," he reported. "It's a bit of a nuisance, isn't it?"

"Well, what are we goin' to do now?" said Douglas. "I *told* you it was goin' to get us into a muddle."

"Well, it's *not* got us into a muddle," said William with spirit. "It's quite an ordn'ry thing for a person

to go out shoppin', isn't it? Everyone goes out
shoppin', don't they?   Well, stands to reason they do,
or there wouldn't be any shops . . .   *Tell* you what!"

"Yes?"

"We'll go and look for him, and you," to the tramp,
"can wait here for him, can't you?   You can go into
his studio an'—sort of start practisin', so's to be
ready for him when we find him.   I bet we don't
take long findin' him.   You don't mind, do you?"

"Not at all," said the tramp genially as he accompanied his new friends into the cottage.

"Look!   Here's the studio," said William, throwing
the door open.

The tramp entered and looked round with interest.

"That's the picture on the easel," said William.

"Oh, yes," said the tramp, appraising the brass
candlesticks on the chimneypiece and deciding that
they wouldn't fetch much.

"Well, we'll go now," said William.   "I don't 'spect
we'll be long findin' him.   You'll be all right, won't
you?"

"Oh, yes, I'll be all right," said the tramp, absently
taking up and examining a spoon that lay on the carpet
—part of the flotsam and jetsam left by Archie's search
for the tea-pot.

"Well, come on then," said William.   He went to
the door, followed by the other Outlaws, then stopped,
struck by a sudden thought.   "Oh, I nearly forgot to
tell you.   There's an awful girl messing about in the
kitchen, but you needn't take any notice of her. . . .
Well, g'bye."

At the gate the four stood for a moment, irresolute.

"He might've gone to Hadley or he might 've gone

to the village," said William, "so let's split up. Ginger
'n' me 'll go an' look for him in Hadley an' you two
go 'n' look for him in the village. I bet he'll be jolly
glad when he finds we've got him a tramp."

"It's a jolly good tramp," said Ginger complacently.

"Yes, we mustn't keep him waitin' too long," said
William, "but, of course, there's lots of things in
Archie's studio, so I 'spect he'll find it int'restin'.'"

William was right. The tramp was finding Archie's
studio extremely interesting. Years of practice as a
picker-up of unconsidered trifles had given him a
quick eye and an unerring judgment. His quick eye
swept the room, coming to rest on the top of the tall
cupboard in which Archie had lately been burrowing.
Between the piles of books and magazines, precariously
stacked there, came a faint gleam of metal. Nimbly
the tramp leapt upon a chair and took down a tarnished
tea-pot. He carried it to the window and examined it.
Solid silver. Good condition. Obviously antique.
Quickly he slipped it into his bundle and made for
the back door. The moment for a hasty and unob-
trusive exit had, he considered, arrived. He opened
the back door, then closed it quickly. A policeman
was strolling idly past the gate. The policeman was
wrapped in his own thoughts—in roseate dreams of
football pool prizes, cinema stars, spectacular promo-
tion to high places at Scotland Yard—and the tramp,
who was a considerate man, did not wish to disturb him.
He stood for some seconds in the tiny passage, waiting,
and, while he waited, there came a sharp series of
knocks at the front door. The tramp glanced from
the back door to the front door, obviously weighing

up the possibilities of escape offered by each. And at that moment the kitchen door opened, and a small tousled head came round it. Beneath the tousled head was a small face streaked with soot and dust. Beneath that was a blackened, waterlogged apron. Despite all this, there was about the whole apparition an impressive air of dignity and self-confidence.

"Go and anthwer the door," it said. "I can't do everything. I'm buthy thpring cleaning."

So peremptory was the voice that, before the tramp quite knew what he was doing, he had slipped his bundle inside the kitchen for safety and was opening the front door.

A middle-aged lady stood there. She was short, but something about her made her look taller than she was. The eyes, behind large rimless glasses, held a gleam of determination. The mouth was set in lines that showed her to belong to the class of those who stand no nonsense.

As she looked at the tramp, an expression of horror spread slowly over her countenance.

"Archibald!" she gasped.

The tramp coughed. He had been in many tight corners in his somewhat colourful career, and he had always found a cough useful. It gave one time to think, to adjust oneself to circumstances, to plan one's next move.

"You don't remember me, of course," went on the lady. "I'm your Aunt Georgina."

The tramp bared his teeth in a smile of welcome. He had decided to take the way of least resistance. The lady, though plainly dressed and not particularly comely, carried with her the indefinable atmosphere of the well-to-do. She was obviously an aunt whom anyone would be glad to possess. The situation held possibilities, and the tramp decided to make what use he could of them in the short time at his disposal.

"Aunt Georgina!" he said on a note of rapture. "Well, fancy me not recognising you! Come on in."

"It would be strange if you did recognise me, Archibald," said the visitor with some asperity as she stepped into the little hall, "considering that we haven't met since your christening."

"Of course, of course," said the tramp. "Fancy me forgetting that! Come in."

He threw open the door of the studio and she entered, eyeing her host with ever-deepening horror.

"But this is dreadful, Archibald," she said at last, as if the words had been torn from her, despite herself, by an emotion too strong to be contained.

"What is, Aunt?" said the tramp, giving her an ingratiating smile.

"Your sister had prepared me for your beard and your—outlandish costume and your general affectation of Bohemianism, but I was not prepared for the depths to which you appear to have sunk."

"Sunk, Aunt?" said the tramp.

"Yes, sunk, Archibald," said Aunt Georgina. "It is not my habit to mince my words or to shirk an unpleasant duty, and I must tell you that your whole appearance shocks me. I realise, of course, that you probably suffer from the artistic temperament."

"Something cruel," said the tramp, introducing a professional whine into his voice. "A little holiday's what the doctor says I need. It wouldn't cost more than a couple o' quid, but——"

Aunt Georgina interrupted him.

"You're practically in rags," she said. "Can't you even afford a decent suit of clothes?"

"I been through some bad times, Aunt," said the tramp, "but I'd like to please you. Now, listen. I'd like to buy a new suit o' clothes in honour of your visit."

"It would certainly be an improvement," said Aunt Georgina, "and I confess that I should like to think that my influence had helped to restore something of your self-respect."

"Well, I'll do it for your sake, Aunt," said the tramp, twisting his villainous features again into the ingratiating smile. "An'—well, I'd treasure them more if I could feel they were your gift to me. Only a couple of quid, lady. I mean, Aunt. I can get a real slap-up new suit fer a couple o' quid."

"Archibald!" gasped Aunt Georgina. "I——" Her gaze wandered to the window. "Who is that young man just coming in at the gate?"

The tramp blenched.

"Well, I'll be off," he said, making for the door. "I got a very important engagement."

"But, Archibald," said Aunt Georgina, "you can't go now with a visitor just arriving at your front door."

"It's the back door I'm goin' by," said the tramp.

He went into the passage, opened the kitchen door, snatched up his bundle and took himself off with such nimbleness that he seemed almost to have vanished into air.

Aunt Georgina sat down weakly and put her hand to her head. Then the door opened and a young man, with a thin harassed face and an armful of paper bags, entered the room.

"Oh, Aunt Georgina," he panted, "I'm so sorry I wasn't here to welcome you."

"Who are you?" said Aunt Georgina faintly.

"I'm Archibald. Your nephew," said Archie.

"Then who," said Aunt Georgina, "was the other?" Archie stared at her in bewilderment.

"What other?" he said.

"Doubtless a joke," said Aunt Georgina. "Ill-timed and in extremely bad taste, but still—— Now let me look at you, Archibald."

Archie let her look at him.

"Well, I must say," continued Aunt Georgina, "it's something of a relief to learn that your humorous friend is not my nephew, after all. No, don't apologise," she went on, misunderstanding the interruption that the bewildered Archie was obviously about to make. "A misplaced sense of humour is, I know, one of the marks of youth, but I think that you're old enough to have outgrown it, Archibald. Now I can only pay you a short visit and I don't want to waste time, so let us discuss this exhibition of your work that your sister says you are anxious to hold in London. I am quite willing to finance it——"

"Oh, Aunt!" said Archie with a gesture of excitement that shed currant buns all over the carpet and sent an iced cake rolling across the floor to settle— iced side down—in the hearth. "How *kind* of you!"

Aunt Georgina raised her hand.

"One moment, Archibald," she said. "I must make sure first that you are worthy of my confidence, that you share my ideals of family obligation." Her eyes went round the room. "Where, Archibald, is the

VIOLET ELIZABETH ENTERED, CARRYING A SILVER
TEA-POT.

silver tea-pot that belonged to your great-great-grand-mother and that I handed on to you as a sacred trust?"

Anxiety and bewilderment returned to Archie's face. He looked desperately around.

"Archibald," said Aunt Georgina portentously, "you've not—you've not *lost* it?"

"No, no," stammered Archie. "No, no, of course not."

He was just on the point of diving into the cupboard again when a diversion was caused by what sounded like a collision between a tank and an express train in the kitchen.

Aunt Georgina started.

"What was that, Archibald?" she said.

Before he could reply another diversion was caused by the clamorous arrival of the Outlaws. Both search parties had missed Archie, but a small boy had informed them of his return and they had come, eager to witness the success of their plan.

"Where's our model?"

"We found you a model, Archie."

"Where's he got to?"

"He was a jolly good one."

"He'd got a beard an' holes in his boots."

"He's got a jolly long waiting list."

"He's in every British Museum in the world."

"Where *is* he?"

"Boys! Boys!" pleaded Archie almost tearfully. "Please don't make so much noise."

The uproar continued.

"He was jolly cheap, Archie."

"Only a bit more than a gard'ner."

"An' mod'lin's skilled work. He said so."

"I bet you can make that tree look like a tramp now."

"Horse."

"Pillar-box."

"Tent."

Aunt Georgina raised a hand.

"*Silence!*" she said.

So quelling were both voice and gesture that the Outlaws were, temporarily, quelled. The uproar died away.

"And *who*," said Aunt Georgina, "are these children?"

Before anyone could answer, the door opened and Violet Elizabeth entered. She carried a silver tea-pot and she gazed round the assembly with an air of authority that rivalled Aunt Georgina's.

"Whereth the gentleman?" she demanded.

"What gentleman?" said Archie.

"He wath here," said Violet Elizabeth, "an' he'd got hith thingth in a little parthel in a handkerchief, and I opened it to thee what he'd got in it and he'd got thith tea-pot in it and it wath all dirty tho I thought I'd clean it for him for a thurprithe tho I did. I put a tin of cocoa in hith parthel for another thurprithe, but—where ith he? I want to give him hith tea-pot all nithe and thining."

They stared at her—except Aunt Georgina, who had seized the tea-pot and was examining it with such absorption that she obviously had not heard a word that Violet Elizabeth had said.

"Oh, Archibald!" she murmured, "how I have misjudged you! I'll confess now that I was beginning to suspect that you had lost or sold it."

Archie blinked and gulped. Events had been moving too quickly for him to keep pace with them, and silence seemed the best policy. Events had been moving too quickly for the Outlaws, too, but silence never seemed the best policy to them.

Oh, shut up about your rotten old tea-pot. Where's our model?"

"I don't know. I've never touthed it. Whereth the gentleman the tea-pot belongth to? I don't want him to mith hith thurprithe."

"He was here when we went. Our model, I mean. What's happened to him."

"I said it would get us into a muddle."

Archie had now gathered together his scattered forces.

"Go away, children," he said. "Go away at once."

Aunt Georgina was still fondling the tea-pot.

"I'm so glad you treasured it, dear boy," she said. "And now let us discuss the arrangements for that exhibition of your work."

"Oh, *Aunt!*" said Archie, his voice tremulous with gratitude.

Aunt Georgina turned to the Outlaws, and it was clear that their dismissal was a matter of seconds. William leapt at his chance. He had no idea what had happened, but there could be no doubt that Archie was back in a good temper again.

"Will you lend us your actin' clothes now, Archie?" he said.

"Certainly," said Archie with a beaming smile.

Violet Elizabeth looked round at the company. Like William, she had no idea what had happened, but the tea-pot seemed to be the key to the situation.

"It wath me that cleaned it," she said in a voice of serene confidence, "tho you'll *have* to let me be Queen Elithabeth now."

CHAPTER II

WILLIAM—THE BOLD

"WHAT about that play you were goin' to write?"
said Ginger.

The Outlaws were whiling away a wet afternoon in
William's bedroom, and—an unusual state of affairs
with them—time hung rather heavy on their hands.

"Oh, yes," said William, brightening. "Yes, I'd
forgot that. Yes, that's a good idea. I'll write it
now. It won't take me long. I'm a jolly quick play
writer."

"Thank goodness we needn't have Violet Elizabeth
for Queen Elizabeth now, anyway," said Ginger.

For, the very day after she had secured the part,
Violet Elizabeth had developed mumps and had withdrawn tempestuously from public life.

"I dunno that I want to have Queen Elizabeth at
all," said William. "She wasn't very int'restin'. She
didn't do anythin' but go trampin' about in puddles
over people's coats. Gosh! I bet they got into rows
when they got home."

"She beat the Armada," said Henry.

"No, she didn't," said William. "Nelson did that."

"Drake."

"Well, Drake, then. But *she* didn't. I 'spect she
jus' swanked about in an A.T.S. uniform, same as
Ethel did in our war, but she didn't do any fightin'. I
don't want to write a play about a woman, anyway.

45

I don't like women an' I don't see why I should write plays about them." He looked at Henry. "Who else was there in hist'ry?"

Henry considered.

"Perkin Warbeck," he said at last.

"What did he do?" said William. "I'm not goin' to write about him if he jus' discovered America or somethin' like that. I'm only goin' to write about him if he did somethin' int'restin' like killin' people."

"Well, he was a rebel," said Henry, "so I bet he killed people."

"All right," said William, "I'll write a play about him an' I'll be him an' the rest of you can be policemen."

"There's got to be a king," said Henry.

"I'll be him, too," said William.

"You can't be the king *an'* the rebel," objected Ginger.

"Yes, I can," said William. "I've acted plays when I've been every single person in them. I've killed someone an' then been the ghost of the person that was killed hauntin' the person that killed him, an' I only got in a bit of a muddle over it. A king an' a rebel's nothin' to me."

"All right," said Ginger. "I'll be the detective."

"I don't think there was a detective in it," said William uncertainly. Again he looked at Henry. "Was there?"

"Well, I don't quite remember," said Henry noncommittally. "There might have been."

"I bet there was," said Ginger. "If he killed people it was a crime, an' there's always a detective in a crime."

"I'll be a ghost," said Douglas, who always liked
to appropriate the less adventurous rôles.

"Whose?" said Henry.

"Anyone's," said Douglas.

"Yes," said William judicially. "All the mos'
excitin' plays have ghosts in 'em. There was one in the
play Shakespeare wrote. He came to dinner an' shook
gory locks at 'em. He was called Scrooge or some such
name."

"What am I goin' to be?" said Henry.

"You can be the army of rebels," said William.
"You can carry that banner your uncle gave you.
It's only a little one, but it's a nice colour."

"It's a naval one," said Henry doubtfully, "an' he
said it meant 'Yellow Fever on Board.'"

"That doesn't matter," said William. "No one can
read banners an', even if they can read it, it makes it
more excitin'."

"But, listen," said Henry. "I've got that new fancy
dress I had for Victor Jameson's fancy dress party.
It's George Washington an' it's got an axe. It's only
cardboard, but it looks like a real one."

"Yes, I remember," said William. "It was jolly good.
All right"—generously—"you can be Perkin Warbeck."

"Well, aren't you goin' to start writin' it?" said
Ginger.

"All right, all right," snapped William. "I've gotter
have time to *think*, haven't I? I've only got one
brain, same as anyone else."

Ginger, anxious not to waste any more time, repressed
the obvious comment, and William, taking from his
pocket a piece of paper so grubby that it could only be
called "blank" by courtesy, and a battered pencil of

the "indelible" variety, lay down on his stomach on the floor (his usual attitude for literary composition), with the paper in front of him, his brow ravelled into the complicated pattern that betokened mental exertion. For some minutes there was no sound but the sound of William's teeth chewing away absently at the point of his pencil, while a tide of purple colouring spread slowly over his features.

"Well, get on," said Henry at last. "Thought you were goin' to write a play about Perkin Warbeck."

"Well, how can I," said William in the tone of one goaded beyond endurance, "with you all goin' on an' on at me all the time? I bet Shakespeare didn't have a lot of people sittin' round him all the time sayin' they thought he was goin' to write a play about Perkin Warbeck."

"All right," said Henry. "We won't say anythin' more. Now get on with it."

Heaving a sigh so long and deep that the paper fluttered several feet away and had to be recaptured, manipulating the pencil carefully so that the fraction of the point that had survived the onset of his teeth could be made to function, William set to work. The others gathered round him, peering over his shoulder.

> seen one pallis king seeted enter perkin warbeck disgized as george washington.
>
> king.   hello george washington cum in I'll ask my mother if thou can stay to tea theres creem buns and sum jelly left over from sundy.

"You see, he doesn't know he's a rebel," explained William in parenthesis. "He thinks he's jus' an ordin'ry visitor."

george washington (throing off disgize). I am not
george washington thou villun I am perkin warbeck
and I hav cum to waid in thy blud.
exit king run after by perkin warbeck with ax.

"Yes, but look," said Henry indignantly. "I can't
throw off the disguise. Not like that—all in a minute
in brackets. That George Washington costume buttons
tight all down me an' it takes hours to get into an'
out of. Besides, there isn't room for anything but my
underclothes underneath it, an' I'd look a jolly silly
rebel jus' in underclothes."

"I do wish you'd stop makin' objections," said
William testily. "Here I am, tryin' to write a great
play, an' all you can do is to go on an' on makin'
objections. All right. Take your rebel clothes with
you in a parcel an' change into them if there's not
room for them under George Washington."

"Yes, an' what's the King goin' to do, while I'm
doin' that? Jus' sit there watchin' me changin' into
my rebel's clothes? That's goin' to look jolly
silly."

"He can be readin' a newspaper," said William,
"an' look as if he couldn't see you."

"Well, it's still goin' to look jolly silly," said Henry.

"When do I come in?" said Ginger anxiously. "I
ought to be on in the first scene lookin' round for
clues."

"There can't be any clues till someone's killed someone," said William. "Use a bit of sense. An'"—with
a fresh burst of irritation—"I wish you'd all stop
crowdin' round me an' breathin' down my neck. How
d'you think great plays like Paradise Lost'd have got

wrote if everyone Shakespeare knew had come crowdin' round him breathin' down his neck?"

The three withdrew to a respectful distance, and William continued his literary efforts.

Seen two a corpse enter rebbles.

Rebbles. Theres a pretty shady corpse over yonder lets sit on it.

The three had gathered round him again.

"What do they want to sit on a dead body for?" said Henry.

"It's *not* a dead body," said William in exasperation. "Corpse means 'wood' in plays an' po'try. An' it's not 'on.' It's 'in.'"

"Why don't you cross your i's, then?" said Henry. "An' I've never come across 'corpse' meanin' 'wood.' It always means 'dead body' in the books I've read."

"Well, you've not read everything, have you?" said William crushingly. "I can't help you bein' so ign'rant that you don't know that 'corpse' means 'wood' in plays an' po'try. If I've got to write plays for people that don't know any English, I might as well stop writin' them altogether, an' I've a jolly good mind to."

"When do I come in?" said Ginger, his anxiety deepening. "Seems to me the play's got about half-way through an' I've not come into it at all yet."

"Anyway, whose *was* this corpse?" said Douglas. "If I've got to be a ghost I ought to know who I'm the ghost of."

"It's a rotten play so far," said Ginger.

"All right, write it yourself," said William, screwing up the piece of paper into a ball and throwing it across the room. "I'm sick of it, an' anyway the pencil's stopped writin', so I couldn't go on with it even if I wanted to." The final abandonment of his literary project seemed to restore his good humour, and he sat up, a thoughtful frown on his face. "You know . . . I think it's time there was another rebellion. There's not been one since the ones in hist'ry. I mean, when people put the days we're livin' in now into hist'ry books in a hundred years' time, it's goin' to be jolly dull without a few rebellions."

The other three considered this point with interest.

"There aren't any rebels," said Douglas, "an' there can't be rebellions without rebels."

"Well, anyone can be a rebel, can't they?" said William impatiently. "Come to that, we could be." He was silent for a few moments while the light that generally heralded one of his ideas broke slowly over his sombre freckled countenance. "Come to that," he went on, "I don't see why we shouldn't be, either."

"We couldn't be," said Douglas. "All the rebels in hist'ry were grown up."

"Well, all the more reason why we should have a turn," said William. "It'd be a change from grown-ups. I think we ought to do somethin' to make hist'ry a bit more int'restin'." He looked at Henry. "What did people rebel about?"

Henry considered.

"'Cause they had grievances," he said.

William gave a short ironic laugh.

"We've got plenty of *them*," he said. "Gosh! when I think of the amount of *them* we've got, it's a wonder we didn't start rebellin' years ago."

"There was a sort of rebellion not very long ago," said Henry thoughtfully. "I heard my father talkin' about it las' week. It was the Irish, an' they rebelled 'cause they'd had their priv'leges took away an' they wanted them back. They used to have a Parliament an' such-like an' they got 'em took away an' they made a rebellion to get 'em back."

"That's what we'll do," said William. "Jus' think of the priv'leges *we've* had took away! Think of the days when children used to work in the mills an' down coal mines an' up chimneys. It mus' have been wizard! I went to a mill once with my uncle an'—gosh! It was grand! Wheels whizzin' round all over the place, an' you put stuff in at one end of a thing an' it came out diff'rent at the other! An' they let me help take somethin' from one place to another in a sort of cage that went whizzin' along the ceiling right high up jus' like an aeroplane. It was abs'lutely *grand*! And jus' *think* of workin' in a place like that every day 'stead of goin' to school—same as children used to in the old days. An' think of goin' down underneath the earth messin' about with coal. An' goin' up chimneys. An' jus' think that children used to do all these things every day till grown-ups stopped them 'cause they didn't want them to have a good time. They wanted us to have a rotten time doin' sums an' French verbs an' g'ography instead."

The Outlaws had frequently heard William give voice to these opinions, but they still found them inspiriting. They gave a murmur of agreement, and William continued.

"Well, now, that's all fixed up. We're goin' to have a rebellion to get back the priv'leges that grown-ups

took off us an' then we're goin' to have a jolly good time
in mills an' up chimneys an' down coal mines."

"How do rebels start?" said Ginger.

"Well, there's got to be a leader," said Henry.

"I'll be him," said William.

"An' this leader's got to rouse followers by makin'
speeches."

"I can do that all right," said William confidently.
"I'm jolly good at makin' speeches. What happens
after that?"

"Didn't you listen to the hist'ry lesson on Monday?"
said Henry.

"No," said William. "I was too busy. I was racin'
my furry caterpillar against Ginger's."

"Mine won," said Ginger.

"It did *not*."

"It did."

"It didn't."

"It did."

"Well, never mind now," said William. "We've
got to get on with this rebellion. Anyway," to Henry,
"what was it about? This hist'ry lesson, I mean."

"It was about a man called Warwick that was a sort
of rebel," said Henry, "an' he captured the King."

William looked slightly taken aback.

"That's goin' to be a bit difficult," he said. "I
mean, the King lives a long way off, an' it'd take us
all day to get to his house, to start with."

"Yes, but there's people that repr'sent him," said
Ginger, "an' if we captured one of those it'd count the
same."

"Who repr'sents him?" said William.

"Well, my aunt gave me a book las' birthday, you

know, called *Civics* or somethin' like that, an' it was so dull that I didn't read it till las' week when I was in bed with that cold an' I felt so mis'rable that I wanted to read a mis'rable book, so I read it."

"An' who did it say repr'sented him?"

"I think it was the army," said Ginger vaguely. "I'm not quite sure, 'cause I was sneezin' all the time, but I think so."

"Well, I don't see how we can capture the army," said William frowning thoughtfully, "not the whole of it, anyway."

"P'raps it wasn't the army," said Ginger. "No, I don't think it was. I think it was the p'lice."

William considered.

"Well, I bet it's no good tryin' to capture the p'liceman here," he said. "He's jolly strong an' jolly bad-tempered. Besides, it wouldn't be excitin' enough, 'cause we know him so well."

"I don't think an ordin'ry p'liceman counts, anyway," said Ginger. "It's got to be someone high-up."

"My father knows a Chief Constable said Henry. "He's called Mr. Wakely an' he's comin' to play chess with my father to-night. Would he do?"

"Yes, I bet he'd do," said Ginger. "I 'spect he's the high-up one round here that repr'sents the King."

"What do we do when we've got him?" said Douglas a little apprehensively.

"Well," said William, considering this for the first time, "I 'spose we send a note to the government sayin' that we won't let him go till they've put our grievances right an' let us go back to mills an' coal mines an' sweepin' chimneys. An' then"—simply—"they will."

"I bet it doesn't turn out as easy as that," said Douglas gloomily.

"I bet it does," said William with spirit. "Of course," he admitted after a slight pause, "there's a few things to get fixed up before we axshully start."

"What'll we do first?" said Ginger.

"We've gotter get an army of rebels together first," said William. "Jus' four rebels isn't enough. They mightn't take any notice of us. It's stopped rainin' so we can start straight away. I'll rouse 'em by makin' a speech, same as you said. We'll have a meetin' an' I bet everyone'll come to it when they know I'm goin' to make a speech."

"I'll bring my trumpet," said Henry.

"I'll bring my drum," said Douglas.

"I'll bring my lasso," said Ginger, "then I can chuck 'em out when they start int'ruptin'."

William took up his stand on a packing-case in the old barn, and the audience drifted slowly in. There was generally an audience when the word had gone round that William was going to make a speech. It wasn't so much the prospect of the actual speech that roused their interest. It was the prospect of the events that usually followed in its train. Life at the moment was a little dull and they welcomed the thought of the excitement that William's projects were apt to infuse into it. The other members of William's gang were there, together with a smattering of village children. Arabella Simpkin, a pugnacious-looking child with red hair, had arrived first, trundling a go-cart in which sat a pugnacious-looking baby with red hair, who brandished a fish slice in the intervals of chewing a raw carrot. Arabella looked round with a contemptuous sniff, then stood, hand on hip, in an attitude copied from her favourite film star. The others straggled in—small boys, small girls, a few toddlers and a couple of dogs.

"Ladies an' gentlemen," began William, "I'm glad you could all come to-day an' I think you're goin' to have a very int'restin' time."

"Speak for yourself," said Arabella Simpkin.

"Shut up!" said William. "Well, now, listen. I'm goin' to make a very int'restin' speech."

The audience raised a ragged cheer. The dogs barked. Arabella gave a high-pitched, sarcastic laugh, rather like a horse's neigh, and the baby hit the nearest toddler on the head with the fish slice.

"Now listen, everyone," said William. "You'd rather work in a mill with big wheels whizzin' round an' things goin' in at one end an' comin' out diff'rent at the other an' riding in carts that go shootin' along the ceiling like aeroplanes, 'stead of goin' to school, wouldn't you?"

"Yes," agreed the audience.

"An' you'd rather be underneath the earth messin' about with coal than do sums an' g'ography, wouldn't you?"

"Yes," agreed the audience.

"An' you'd like to go sweepin' chimneys an' messin' about with soot an' stuff, wouldn't you?"

"*Yes!*" shouted the audience.

"Well, those are our priv'leges that got took off us an' we've got to get 'em back an' the only way we can get 'em back is by bein' rebels. D'you want to be rebels?"

"YES!" roared the audience.

"Well, then, you're a rebel army an' I'm the leader an' we've got to capture someone that's the same as the King an' then they'll have to let us all go back to havin' a good time bein' chimney sweeps an' such-like."

"Won't make much diff'rence to you, far as your face goes," said Arabella with a snort.

"You shut up," said William, passing a hand over that member. "My face is all right."

"Might be if you could see it," retorted Arabella, "but I doubt it."

"Well, shut up, anyway."

"No, I won't shut up, either. 'S a free country, isn't it? I can say what I like, can't I?"

"You'd've got your head cut off in hist'ry, carryin' on like this," said William sternly.

"All right, you try it," challenged Arabella. "You jus' try cuttin' my head off."

Ginger made an effort to lasso her, but the loop caught Douglas round his shoulders and brought him down on top of the red-haired baby, who began to belabour him with carrot and fish slice.

"Now listen," said William, raising his voice above the uproar. "You're a rebel army an' you've got to get weapons—bows an' arrows an' pistols an' pokers an' things—an' you've got to come when I blow this whistle (he took a whistle from his pocket and blew a piercing blast) 'cause that's the sign for the rebellion to start. See?"

Henry blew his trumpet, Douglas beat his drum. Ginger began to sing "God Save the King," then stopped abruptly, realising that it was hardly appropriate to the occasion. Arabella Simpkin took the baby's carrot and threw it at William, hitting him neatly in the eye, the baby began to howl, the dogs began to fight, and the meeting broke up in general disorder.

But William, walking home with the Outlaws, felt well satisfied with his afternoon's work.

"We've got an army," he said. "All we have to do now is to capture this Mr. Wakely."

"Yes," said Douglas, "an' if you think that's goin' to be easy——"

"We'll prob'ly have to use a bit of cunnin'," said William, "but if that other rebel leader could do it, I don't see why I shouldn't. Anyway, I'm goin' home to tea now an' I'll have a think about it while I'm havin' tea."

The only other members of his family present at tea were Mrs. Brown and Ethel. Ethel, it seemed, had been to London with Jimmy Moore the day before and had found the expedition unsatisfactory.

"You'd think taxis hadn't been invented," she was saying bitterly. "You'd think it was a treat to stand in a bus queue. Wouldn't you have thought he'd have had the sense to book a table for lunch? But—oh, no! We trailed about from place to place and found everywhere full and had to have lunch in a ghastly hole with dead flowers on the table and darns in the table-cloth and only rabbit left."

"Well, what's wrong with rabbit?" said William. He gave a short sinister laugh. "People have to live on worse things than rabbit in rebellions. Rats, I shouldn't be surprised."

"Don't talk such nonsense, dear," said Mrs. Brown. She looked at his features, which could be dimly

discerned beneath their covering of indelible pencil.
" And what *have* you got on your face ? "

"Pencil," said William simply, "an' I did wash it."

"It doesn't look as if you had."

"No, it's that sort of pencil. It's one of those
indelicate ones."

Mrs. Brown gave a helpless sigh and turned again to
Ethel.

"But you saw a nice film, didn't you, dear?"

"Oh, yes," said Ethel indifferently, "but it wasn't
the one I'd wanted to see. More bus queues. More
trailing about. And then we just had to go where
we could get a seat."

Again Mrs. Brown sighed.

"But he's such a nice boy."

"I know," said Ethel. "That's what makes me so
mad. He's asked me to go up with him again next
Saturday, but I've told him I'd rather die. Anyway,
Colonel Maidstone will be home on Friday and I've
promised to go up with him to a dinner and dance on
Saturday. He knows how to do things properly."

"Y-yes," said Mrs. Brown, "but I don't like him
as much as I like Jimmy."

"Neither do I," said Ethel, "but he does know how
to take one out. Taxis, tables booked, sprays of car-
nations, stalls . . . Everything goes like clockwork
and is wonderful. It makes me feel like someone on
the films."

William automatically accorded this statement a
snort of derision, but it was an absent-minded snort.
His thoughts had turned to Colonel Maidstone—a
quiet, retiring middle-aged man who had recently taken
The Limes furnished and had attached himself to the

Brown household, playing golf with Mr. Brown and paying marked attentions to Ethel. William had not till now taken much notice of him, but it suddenly occurred to him that he might be useful. . . . He frequently found Ethel's admirers useful. They were apt to labour under the delusion that to ingratiate themselves with William helped to win Ethel's favour, and a certain amount of advantage could generally be wrung from the situation before they realised their mistake. Stretching out his hand absently for his fifth sandwich (for anxiety never impaired William's appetite), he continued to give the conversation his close attention.

"It was awfully good of him to let us keep the tennis tea things in his garage while he's away," said Ethel.

William remembered that the tennis pavilion had been undergoing repairs and that Ethel had been using Colonel Maidstone's garage as a parking place for the tea equipment in his absence.

"I hope you haven't lost the key," said Mrs. Brown.

"Oh, no," smiled Ethel. "I keep it on a string pinned to the pocket of my big coat, so that I can't forget where I've put it. He's got another, of course, so it wouldn't be fatal if I did lose it. And we moved the things back to the pavilion this morning."

"Where has he gone to?" said Mrs. Brown. "France, isn't it?"

"No, Italy," said Ethel. "His sister's a contessa there, and he often goes over to see her." She sighed. "It's terribly thrilling and romantic. We've never had anyone half so exciting living in the village before."

Then they both became aware of William watching and listening with an intensity that made them vaguely uneasy. Experience had taught them that when William's face wore that particular expression, strange and unexpected things were wont to happen.

"Now, William, this is nothing to do with you," said Mrs. Brown. "If you've finished your tea, go out."

William had finished his tea. He went out. His brow was corrugated with thought, his eyes gleamed with purpose. For suddenly he saw his way clear before him. The actual capture of the King's representative had never presented much difficulty to his mind, but the place of detention had been causing him a certain amount of anxiety. How could they keep their captive so that he should not be immediately discovered and rescued? And Colonel Maidstone's garage seemed to be the answer to the problem. It was empty, the key could easily be detached from Ethel's pocket, and—best of all—Colonel Maidstone was one of Ethel's admirers and so must perforce endure without retaliation whatever inconveniences might result from the unofficial requisitioning of his premises. Moreover, Mr. Wakely, the "King's representative," was coming to play chess with Henry's father that very night. The stage was set. The train was laid. The standard of rebellion could now openly be raised. There were probably a few points that would still need adjusting, but they could be adjusted as they arose.

It was a fine night, and Mr. Wakely, Chief Constable of the County, had decided to walk the few miles from Hadley to the village. He strolled slowly along the pleasant country road, stopping as he reached the outskirts of the village, to compare his watch with the church clock. It was then that he became aware

"ALL THOSE PRIV'LEGES THAT WERE TOOK OFF US,"
SAID WILLIAM. "THEY'VE GOTTER COME BACK."

of a motley band of children following him. They carried bows and arrows, toy pistols, rolling-pins, pokers, stair-rods.... One wore a Red Indian costume, another a pirate's costume, another a bus conductor's uniform. One had a saucepan on his head, another a tea cosy. One walked slowly and with difficulty, encased in a fire-guard. Another brandished a cricket stump. One held aloft a rusty potato masher of ancient design. Another carried a bedraggled banner on the end of a broomstick, while another made ferocious passes at the air with a tin-opener as he walked. Mr. Wakely smiled at them benignly and stood aside to let them pass. They hung back, unwilling, apparently, to take precedence of him.

Still smiling benignly, Mr. Wakely continued on his way. Nice to see the little fellows enjoying themselves at their childish games, he thought. . . . Then he became aware of two boys, walking on either side of him. One was a boy with a shock of untidy red hair. The other was a stocky boy whose brows were drawn into a ferocious scowl and who walked with an assumption of dignity oddly at variance with a purple-streaked face, stockings that had sagged over his shoes (the garters were in his pocket ready for use as catapults should the need arise) and a tie worn at an unusual angle. He recognised them as school friends of Henry's and turned his benign smile on them, happily unaware that he had been captured by a rebel army and was being marched to a place of imprisonment.

"Now, let me see . . ." he said genially. "I know you, of course, but I've forgotten your names."

"William," said one shortly, and "Ginger," said the other.

"Yes, yes, of course. I remember now. Friends of Henry's, aren't you? Lovely evening, isn't it?"

"'S all right for people that can enjoy it," said William. "People that can work in mills an' sweep chimneys."

Mr. Wakely looked at him in pardonable surprise.

"Er—what did you say, my boy?" he said, thinking that he had not heard aright.

"All those priv'leges that were took off us," said William earnestly. "They've gotter come back. We're same as the ones in hist'ry, but the King lives too far off an' anyway you're the same as him, aren't you? That mill I once went over was wizard. An' I bet *you'd* rather go up chimneys an' go shootin' across a ceilin' than do sums. An' it's all been took off us, an' we've got to get it back."

Mr. Wakely's bewilderment was increasing.

"I'm afraid I don't quite follow," he said. "Perhaps . . ."

They had reached the gate of Colonel Maidstone's house. William and Ginger stopped short. Mr. Wakely, finding his way barred by the two boys, stopped short. The whole procession stopped short. It occurred to William suddenly and for the first time that the imprisoning of his captive might be rather a tricky business. Mr. Wakely, in real life, looked larger and more powerful that he had looked in William's imagination of the scene.

He nodded his head in the direction of the garage and spoke in a tone that was intended to be ingratiating, but that actually suggested an acute attack of laryngitis.

"Wouldn't you like to go in there an' have a nice rest?" he said. "I 'spect you're feelin' a bit tired, aren't you, an' it's jolly comfortable in there."

"No, thank you," said Mr. Wakely. "I think perhaps I'd better be getting on."

William quickly turned to other tactics.

"Listen," he said earnestly. "There's somethin' in that garage we want you to see particular. It's somethin' jolly important. It's somethin' you *ought* to see. It's somethin' you'll be sorry all the rest of your life if you don't see. It's somethin'—well, it's somethin' you've *got* to see, isn't it, Ginger?"

"Yes," said Ginger.

Mr. Wakely looked from one to the other. There was something strangely convincing in their earnestness. In any case he was a little early for his game of chess with Henry's father and it would do no harm to while away a few minutes joining in their childish games. He walked up the short drive with William on one side, Ginger on the other and the rebel army in the rear. William took out a key and opened the door. Mr. Wakely stepped inside. Quick as lightning William slammed the door and turned the key. But in the moment of slamming the door, he had seen something that puzzled and surprised him. Colonel Maidstone's car was back in the garage. Evidently he had returned from Italy earlier than he had expected. This, of course, complicated a situation that was far from simple to start with, but, William decided with a shrug, there was nothing he could do about it. At any rate, he had led his rebel army to victory. The King's representative was safely captured and imprisoned.

He stood listening outside the garage for a few moments, but there was no sound from within—no shouts of anger, no threats or appeals for help—only a strange and disconcerting silence. He walked down to the gate, where his rebel army awaited him.

"Ladies an' gentlemen," he said, giving a military

QUICK AS LIGHTNING WILLIAM SLAMMED
THE DOOR.

salute, "we've captured the King's repr'sentative an'
that means we've won the war."

A ragged cheer rose from the ranks.

"Now you can all go home," continued William,

"while we get things fixed up, an' you can come along later an' see what's happened an' when you can stop goin' to school an' start chimney sweepin' an' such-like."

Another cheer arose. The little boy in the bus conductor's uniform turned head over heels. The little boy with the potato masher started a fight with the little boy in the fire-guard. The little boy with the stair-rod, who was extremely vague about the whole thing, began to sing "Good King Wenceslas" and was extinguished by the little boy with the tea cosy.

"Well, you'd better go now," said William, who was beginning to feel slight—very slight—qualms about the whole business. "If you don't go quick, we may not be able to get it fixed up so's you can start cleanin' chimneys an' goin' down coal mines first thing on Monday mornin'."

With another cheer the rebel army straggled off. The four Outlaws (Henry had concealed himself in the ranks of the rebel army in order not to be recognised by the captive) stood at the gate, looking apprehensively at the garage door. The strange silence continued.

"Well, come on," said William. "The nex' thing we've got to do is to write a letter to the gov'nment, tellin' them we've captured him, an' that we'll only let him out if they'll promise to give us back our old priv'leges, sweepin' chimneys an' workin' in mills an' such-like."

"Why's he so quiet?" said Henry with an uneasy glance at the garage door.

"P'raps he's died of fright," said Douglas gloomily, "then we'll all get hung for murder."

"Oh, shut up," said William impatiently. "It's

you that's more likely to die of fright. We've won
the war an' you go on grousin' an' grumblin' as if we'd
lost it. I 'spect he's quiet 'cause he's fed up at gettin'
conquered so easy. You'd be fed up if you'd got
conquered as easy as that. Come on. Let's go to
Ginger's house 'cause it's nearest, an' write the letter."

The letter was composed by William, lying full-length
on his stomach in Ginger's bedroom.

Deer guvvernment [it read],

  Weve conkered the kings reppersentative an
put him in prizon but weel let him out if you prommis
to give us bak our old privledges. If you dont we will
waid in your blud for our rites.

       Yours truely,
    William Brown and the rebble army.

"There!" said William. "That's a jolly good letter.
I bet it scares them. Come on. We'll address it to
the P'lice Station, Hadley, 'cause it's the p'lice that
repr'sents the King an' we'll take it to Hadley an'
post it so's it'll get to them quick."

"Yes, an' who's got a stamp?" said Douglas
sarcastically.

"You don't need a stamp when you write to the
gov'nment," said William. "You mus' be jolly ign'rant
not to know that. They put the stamp on themselves
at the other end."

"Why?"

"Well, it gives 'em somethin' to do. . . . Oh, come
on an' stop wastin' time."

They trooped into Hadley, posted the letter, then
returned by the short cut across the fields. Beneath

WILLIAM STOOD GLUED TO THE SPOT WITH AMAZEMENT.

their natural exhilaration at having brought the affair to such a satisfactory conclusion was a faint under-current of anxiety. The whole thing seemed too simple to be true.

"Gosh! There's one thing I never thought of," said William suddenly. "We've got to take some food to him. We can't let him starve to death."

"Why not?" said Ginger. "They did in hist'ry."

"Yes, but I nearly starved to death myself once," said William, "so I know what it's like. I once went without food from breakfast till nearly tea-time 'cause

it was a picnic an' we'd forgot the basket. All that
time I only had some sweets an' ice cream an' a few
apples an' biscuits, so I know what it's like to nearly
starve to death an' I don't want even a villain an'
tyrant like him to do it."

"That's all very well," said Henry, "but how can we
get him food?"

"Well, there's half an apple turnover in our larder,"
said William, "an' I bet I can find some bits in the
chicken bucket that aren't too bad. I've et bits out
of the chicken bucket myself when I've been rav'nous
with hunger. Bits of cheese an' pastry an' crusts an'
things. They tasted jolly good."

"Yes, an' who's goin' to take it to him?" said
Douglas. "He's prob'ly so mad with rage he'll kill you
soon as he sees you."

"No, I 'spect he'll be so hungry he won't think of
it," said William. "Anyway, I'll jus' open the door
an' shove it in an' then shut the door quick before he's
time to get at me."

"Well, I'll be jolly s'prised if you come out alive,"
said Douglas.

"Oh, will you?" said William. "Well, I'll be jolly
s'prised if I don't. . . . Come on. I've got to get that
apple turnover an' those bits from the chicken bucket
before it gets dark. An' you'd better not come with
me. My family might start gettin' suspicious if we
all went together. They start gettin' suspicious jolly
quick, do my family."

He made his way home, took the apple turnover
from the larder, filled his pockets with the more edible
portion of the chicken scraps and was tiptoeing across
the hall past the half-open door of the sitting-room,

when he saw a sight that held him as if glued to the spot by amazement. For there, standing on the hearth-rug, large, genial, unperturbed, stood Mr. Wakely, Chief Constable, the King's representative, whom William had left safely imprisoned in Colonel Maidstone's garage not half an hour before. Mrs. Brown, Ethel and Jimmy Moore sat round him, listening to him with expressions of eager interest. None of them noticed William.

"Yes, the kids put me on to it," Mr. Wakely was saying. "How they found it out is a mystery, but they told me that there was something in the garage that I ought to see, so in I went."

"Rather trusting of you," said Jimmy.

"Oh, I don't know. I could see they weren't pulling my leg. They were obviously in earnest and I'm an inquisitive man by nature, you know. Anyway I saw a car there and—well, as the kids had warned me that there was something fishy in the place, I took a good look at it. I've got a rather observant eye, and the first thing I noticed was that the upholstery of the car was covered with dirty covers but that they were sewn on with clean cotton and I wondered why. So I poked around a bit and finally took them off and investigated the upholstery and, to cut a long story short, there were over a thousand pairs of nylons hidden in the stuffing of the seats and arms and back."

"And he never gave me one," said Ethel with a wail of anguish.

"They were smuggled, young woman," said Mr. Wakely.

"I shouldn't have minded that," sighed Ethel.

"You mean—he's a black marketeer?" said Mrs. Brown.

"Oh, yes. We've been on to Scotland Yard, and, if it's the man they think it is, they've been trying to get him for some time. He's gone up to London to-day to fix things up with the rest of the gang, I suppose. We've got someone waiting at the station for him now."

"Oh, dear!" said Ethel. "He was so charming and aristocratic. I simply can't believe it. A colonel with a sister who's an Italian contessa!"

Mr. Wakely smiled.

"He's not a colonel and his sister isn't a contessa," he said.

"He seemed so fond of me," said Ethel with a far-away look in her eyes.

"That's his technique, if he's the man they're after," said Mr. Wakely. "He takes a furnished house in the country and attaches himself to the most ordinary and innocuous family in the neighbourhood (the Browns tried not to flinch at this), as a sort of family friend and if there's an attractive unmarried daughter he pays marked attention to her. Then there's no mystery about him. He's accepted as an ordinary member of the community, and no one wonders why he's there or what he's doing. Smuggling, of course, is only a side-line, but he does quite a lot of it, and he's an expert at vanishing without leaving a trace. At the last place where he lived he posed as a naval commander, and he vanished in a night so completely that Scotland Yard have lost track of him ever since."

"But do you mean to say that it was William who told you about him?" said Mrs. Brown incredulously.

"Yes. That's really what I came along for. To thank him and ask how he got on to it. Sorry he's out."

Then suddenly they turned to see William standing in the doorway.

"Oh, there you are, dear," said Mrs. Brown. "Come on in."

William came on in. His face wore the look of wooden imbecility that it was wont to assume in times of crisis. The hand that clutched the remains of the apple turnover was held rigidly behind his back.

"Congratulations, young man!" said Mr. Wakely "I don't know what made you suspect the fellow, but you and your pals have done a fine piece of detective work. You made one mistake, however. You were quite right in shutting the garage door on me, because naturally one didn't want a crowd of onlookers, but what you didn't realise, my boy, was that when you locked them out you locked me in."

He laughed heartily. William blinked, gulped and bared his teeth in a glassy smile.

"However, I got out quite easily by the window," went on Mr. Wakely, "but what made you suspect him in the first place?"

They all looked at William expectantly. He maintained his glassy smile with an effort.

"Well, I can't quite remember jus' at the minute," he said vaguely. "I jus' sort of forget. I mean——"

At that point the apple turnover that he was holding behind his back disintegrated and fell with a" plop!" on to the carpet.

"Oh, William!" groaned Mrs. Brown. "If you were

hungry, why didn't you *ask* for it and eat it in the kitchen? What on earth was the object of carrying it about with you?"

William glanced at the "object," who still stood on the hearth-rug smiling at him benignly, then plunged desperately into an explanation.

"Well, I sort of took it 'cause—well, I thought I might—might meet a hungry person. You never know when you're goin' to meet a hungry person an'—an'—well, it's nice to have a bit of somethin' to give 'em if you do, jus'—jus'—jus' to stop 'em starvin' to death."

"William, what *nonsense*!"

Mrs. Brown had seized the coal shovel and was gathering up the fragments of apple turnover. William bent down to help her, sending a small cascade of cheese rinds and crusts from the pocket where he had secreted the chicken scraps.

"William!" gasped Mrs. Brown, "what on *earth* have you got those chicken scraps for?"

"He thought he might meet a hungry hen," suggested Ethel.

"Yes, that was it," said William, grateful for the explanation. "I'm—I'm jolly fond of hens an'—an' it mus' be rotten for a hen—bein' hungry, I mean—I mean, jus' think of bein' shut up in a prison slowly starvin' to death."

"William, *who's* shut up in a prison?" said Mrs. Brown in exasperation, removing a piece of cheese rind from her shoe.

"This King's repr'sentative. I mean, this hen . . . I mean—well, I bet Perkin Warbeck did worse things than take a few scraps out of his mother's chicken

bucket jus' to stop Mr. Wakely starvin' to death . . .
I mean, this hen . . . I mean . . ."

He gave it up and took refuge again in his glassy
smile.

Under cover of William's eloquence, Jimmy had
turned to Ethel.

"You will come up to town with me on Saturday,
won't you, Ethel?"

"Yes, Jimmy," said Ethel with a sigh.

"Thanks," said Jimmy, his voice hoarse with gratitude. "I'll do things differently, Ethel. I promise
I will. I'll have taxis everywhere even if I have to
buy one of the darn things and I'll book a table at a
decent place. . . ."

Mr. Wakely had taken out his note-case and was
handing a ten-shilling note to William.

"That's a slight expression of my own personal
gratitude, my boy," he said. "And now, tell me what
put you on the fellow's track?" He looked at the
clock and gave a start. "Good Heavens! Is that
right? I ought to be at the station by now. . . . Well,
we'll go into all that later, my boy, and I shall look
forward to hearing your story. Good-bye for the
present."

When he had gone, Mrs. Brown, Ethel and Jimmy all
turned to William.

"Now tell us, William," said Mrs. Brown, "how did
you discover that this man was a criminal?"

William looked out of the window and gave a start.
His army of rebels was marching down the road towards
the house—banner flying, potato masher, stair-rod,
poker well in evidence. William had told them to
come along later to see what had happened, and they

were coming along later to see what had happened. About twenty of them. He glanced down at the ten-shilling note in his hand. A sixpenny ice cream each. They'd be disappointed about the result of the rebellion, of course, but a sixpenny ice cream can salve most disappointments.

"Yes, do tell us, William," said Ethel. "It was rather wonderful of you."

"I should think it was," said Jimmy.

William looked at them thoughtfully. Their attitude was flattering, of course, but it would not, he knew, survive a knowledge of the facts of the case. A knowledge of the facts of the case might even imperil his newly-found wealth.

He went to the door, turned there to say, "All right, I'll tell you. I'll tell you after I've bought the ice creams," then ran quickly out to meet his rebel army, waving his ten-shilling note exultantly aloft.

CHAPTER III

WILLIAM AND THE BROWN CHECK SPORTS COAT

"IT'S jolly rotten," said William bitterly. "Fancy callin' this a free country! Well, it jus' makes me laugh when I hear people callin' it a free country."

To prove his words he uttered a hollow laugh, suggestive of a corn-crake's note, then resumed his expression of deep melancholy.

"It serves you right," said Robert, with elder brother severity. "You think you can go messing up other people's property with impunity, and it's time you learnt that you can't."

"I haven't messed up anyone's prop'ty with that thing you said," replied William indignantly. "I haven't got one, so I can't have. An' if it means makin' fires, we've never even made one in the Little Wood."

Robert sighed hopelessly.

"It's impossible to talk to you," he said. "No wonder father says you can't speak English."

"It's the King's English he says I can't speak," said William. "I can speak my own all right. And I think it's jolly mean to take our short cut an' the Little Wood away from us."

"Personally," said Robert, "all my sympathies are with General Moult."

William, who had liked the sound of his hollow laugh, repeated it.

"They would be," he said. "Grown-ups always stick together. It's a rotten field, anyway, but it was a good short cut to Ginger's, an' it had the Little Wood at the end. We'd got some jolly good games for the Little Wood, an' no one ever stopped us goin' there till Gen'ral Moult bought it, an' he only wants it to keep his ole hen-houses in. We wouldn't do his ole hen-houses any harm. *Or* his ole hens. We aren't int'rested in hens, an' I can't understand a man what's lived in Africa an' known lions an' zebras an' ostriches an' things bein' int'rested in hens, either. It shows his brain mus' be goin'—if he ever had one to go."

This neat piece of sarcasm pleased William so much that a certain complacency invaded his gloom and he repeated it with modest pride: "If he ever had one to go," adding, "An' I jolly well don't think he ever did have one. He oughter be in a lunatic asylum."

"You should know about that," said Robert cryptically. "Anyway, he's written a very strong letter to father and you just can't go there any more, so it's no good talking about it."

"I never thought it was any good," said William with dignity, "but I don't see why I shouldn't talk about it if I want to. Same as father talkin' about the Gov'nment an' you talkin' about the laundry spoilin' your pink shirt an' mother talkin' about queues. People can talk about what they like, can't they?"

"Well, you'll have to talk about it to yourself, then," said Robert, "because I'm going off to cricket now."

The telephone bell rang, and Robert went into the house to answer it. William remained in the garden, hands dug deeply into his pockets, brows drawn together in a frown, ruminating on his wrongs.

"Everythin' gets took off us," he said, fixing a stern eye upon the nearest object, which happened to be the bird bath. "When it's not bows an' arrows an' pocket money, it's woods an' fields an' things. They seem to get meaner an' meaner every day, do grown-ups."

Then he remembered that his bow and arrows had been restored to him that morning by his father after a fortnight's compulsory retirement due to a broken garden frame and, despite himself, something of his natural cheerfulness returned to him. "But it doesn't make up for that field," he muttered, clinging to his grievances. "Nothin' could make up for that field."

The field at the back of General Moult's house was bounded by a spinney that had lately been the scene of most of the Outlaws' activities. There was a pine tree that formed the mast of their pirate ship and from which they could look out over uncharted seas. . . . There was an elm tree whose lower branches formed seats in which the Outlaws could recline in comfort with bottles of lemonade and such refreshments as could safely be abstracted from their home larders. . . . Between the hedge and a tall, thick bramble bush they had made a leafy hide-out in which they were invisible from all sides, and which formed a convenient refuge from real or imaginary foes. The news that General Moult had bought this piece of land and was determined to put a stop to trespassing had been a staggering blow to them.

"Him and his South Africa!" muttered William, addressing himself now to a dandelion that had eluded

Robert's haphazard week-end "weeding" and flourished brazenly in the top niche of the rockery. "Him and his South Africa! You'd think that anyone what was as keen on South Africa as what he thinks he is, wouldn't grudge other people a bit of ole felt. . . . That's what they call fields in South Africa," he explained, a little self-consciously, turning his frowning gaze to a stone frog that had been given to his sister Ethel on her last birthday by a boy friend and that seemed to be staring at him inquiringly from a cluster of nasturtiums.

"You going to be in this afternoon, William?" said Robert, coming out of the house.

"No, I'm goin' to meet Ginger an' the others at the ole barn," said William.

"Oh." Robert glanced at his watch. "Well, I've got a man coming about that coat."

"What coat?" said William.

Again Robert sighed hopelessly.

"Do you ever listen to *anything*?" he said. "I was talking about it at lunch."

"I've got other things to do at lunch than listenin' to you talkin'," said William loftily. "I was pretendin' that I was shipwrecked on a raft, an' that that mince was the last ship's biscuit left."

"You certainly wolfed it up as if you were starving," said Robert, "but then you usually do." He was tempted to enlarge on the theme of William's table manners, but realised that this was no moment for hostilities and continued more pacifically: "Anyway, you know I've been selling some clothes, don't you?"

Robert, on being demobilised, had discovered, to his dismay, that the war, in addition to disorganising the entire universe, had put two inches on to his chest measurement and that few of his pre-war coats could now be worn with comfort. "It's not that I've grown fat," he was careful to explain to his friends, "it's that I'm more muscular."

"Yes," said William. "I know you sold that ole overcoat las' week an' that the man what bought it said it was a bit noisy, but that it took all sorts to make a world."

"The word was 'loud,' not 'noisy'," said Robert coldly. "And actually the thing was in perfect taste, but that's not the point. The point is that I put an advertisement of my brown check sports coat in the paper shop in Hadley yesterday, and someone's just rung up to say that he's coming to see it, and that he'll be here at two. Well, the cricket practice starts at two, so you see it's a bit awkward."

William saw that it was . . . Ethel and Mrs. Brown had gone to London for the day, and Mr. Brown was at the office.

"I'll see to it for you, Robert," he offered. "I needn't go to the old barn till after two."

Robert looked at him with a distrust born of long and bitter experience.

"I've never known you see to anything yet," he said, "without making a mess of it."

"I could tell you hundreds of things I've not made a mess of," said William.

"All right," challenged Robert. "Tell me one."

"I can't think of one jus' at the moment," admitted William, "but I bet I could if you gave me time."

"You'd need a lifetime," said Robert, "and even then there'd be something phoney about it."

"Oh, all right," said William distantly, "if you don't want me to . . ."

"Yes, I do want you to," said Robert hastily. "It's all right. I do want you to. I'll give you sixpence if you do it without making a mess of it."

"Gosh! Thanks *awfully*," said William.

"Now listen carefully," said Robert. "This chap —his name's Mr. Cooper—is coming at two, and all you have to do is to give him my brown check sports coat and take ten bob from him. Don't take a half-penny less than ten bob."

"I don't see that a halfpenny makes all that differ-ence," said William the literal. "S'pose he offers nine and elevenpence halfpenny?"

"Ten bob," said Robert firmly. "Ten bob or nothing. Well, I must be getting along now. . . . He'll be here by two, and then you can run off to Ginger and the others."

He went into the hall, took up his cricket bag, and strode down to the gate. At the gate he turned.

"Not a halfpenny less than ten bob, mind," he said. "And if you make a mess of it you can jolly well look out for yourself."

"That's all right, Robert," said William easily. "There's nothin' for you to worry about."

Robert vanished down the road, and William turned again to the bird bath.

"Gosh!" he said, with a short, amused laugh. "Anyone'd think I hadn't any sense, the way they go on. Fancy thinkin' that someone what's dived into rivers from aeroplanes goin' at top speed, an' captured whole tribes of Red Indians an' rounded up whole gangs of crim'nals can't sell an ole coat. . . ." He paused for a few moments, remembering that the exploits he had just enumerated had been largely imaginary, and ended somewhat lamely: "Anyway, I bet anyone can sell an ole coat, whether he's done things like that or not."

He went into the hall to look at the clock. Ten to two. The man was coming for the coat at two. . . . Well, he'd get the coat and have it ready. He went to the tool shed, took the well-worn brown check sports coat from its hook behind the pile of beezums, and put it on the chair in the hall. Eight minutes to two. Gosh! It was a jolly long ten minutes. It was goin' to be worth a bit more than sixpence hanging round like this all afternoon. He decided to renew acquaintance with his recently-restored bow and arrows. "But it was a rotten bad shot," he said gloomily, as he brought it out into the garden. "Some of 'em are. Mine always seem to be. This one'd broke two windows an' the garden frame that first day before father took it off me, an' I was aimin' at somethin' diff'rent each time. There mus' be somethin' wrong with the balance." He threw a frowning speculative glance round the garden. "I'll aim at that tree an' I bet I hit it all right. I *bet* I hit it. . . . That tree's a enemy tribe's council of war, an' they don't know I'm here. It's a jolly dangerous thing to do. . . . I'll be jolly lucky if I escape with my life."

He crept a little nearer the tree under cover of a watering can that Robert had left on the lawn, took long and careful aim and shot. The arrow vanished, and at once the air was rent by loud and discordant squawkings.

"IS THIS FER ME?" SAID THE MAN.   "THANK YOU
KINDLY, YOUNG SIR."

"Gosh!" said William, aghast.   "Killed one of her
ole hens, I shouldn't wonder."

He crouched behind the summer house, but no
indignant next-door face appeared over the fence, and
he remembered with relief having seen its owner
setting out immediately after lunch with a shopping
basket.   He approached the fence and peeped across
it. . . .   The arrow had embedded itself harmlessly
in the centre of the chicken run, and the chickens
were running round it in that state of moral dis-
integration to which their kind is prone.   He picked
up a twig, conveniently shaped like a pistol, climbed
over the fence and advanced into the chicken run,
hunching up his shoulders in a manner suggestive of a
Hollywood gangster, and moving the pistol quickly
from side to side, making short sharp clicking sounds
with his tongue as he did so, to mark the ceaseless flow

of the unerring bullets. Then he seized his arrow, brandished it exultantly above his head, and climbed back into his own garden.

"Ha-ha!" he taunted the still demoralised fowls. "Twenty to one against me and not one of you could stop me rescuing my trusty tomahawk. Poltroons and cowardy-custards——"

He turned suddenly to find a man standing on the garden path watching him. Gosh! thought William. The man for Robert's coat! I'd almost forgotten it. . . .

"That was pretty good," said the man. "Made 'em sit up, all right, didn't you?"

William grinned. "Yes, I jolly well did," he agreed. "I won't be a minute gettin' the coat."

He ran into the house, brought out the coat, and thrust it into the man's arms.

"There you are," he said.

It occurred to him on closer inspection that the man was a very shabby man. But then, the coat was a very shabby coat. . . .

"That fer me?" said the man.

He had an unshaven face, a husky voice, and a jovial eye. William took a liking to him. He decided that he should have the coat for nine and eleven-pence halfpenny if he wanted it, and that he, William, would make up the odd halfpenny.

"Yes," said William. "It's Robert's coat."

"Not arf bad, neither," said the man. "Thank you kindly, young sir. A coat same as this 'ere was just wot I wanted."

"Your name *is* Mr. Cooper, isn't it?" said William.

"Oh, yes," agreed the man, after a few seconds' hesitation. "Me name's Cooper, all right."

"Well, Robert wants ten shillings for the coat. It said so on the advertisement, didn't it?"

"Y-yes," said the man thoughtfully. "Ten shillin's. That were it, weren't it?"

"And Robert had to go to cricket, so he left me to see to it. I told him it'd be all right. He's only been gone a few minutes, but his cricket practice started at two, you see, so he couldn't wait. But he said that if you gave me the ten shillings you could take the coat."

"Yes, so he told me," said the man.

"Oh, you know Robert, do you?" said William, surprised.

"'Course I knows Robert. Robert an' me's ole friends. I ought to've told you at the beginnin' that I met 'im at the end of the road an' giv 'im the ten bob fer the coat an' 'e said jus' to cut along an' get it an' tell the nipper it were all right about the ten bob."

"Oh," said William.

"But I thought I wouldn't tell you till I'd seen 'ow you 'andled the job, an' I mus' say you 'andled it in a proper business-like way an' no mistake. I'll tell Robert so when nex' I see 'im."

William's heart swelled with pride.

"Oh, I can manage things all right, really," he said airily. "I'm jolly good at managing things really. It's only that they've got a sort of idea that I'm not, that's all."

"They'll 'ave a pretty diff'rent idea after this," said the man. "'Andled it good an' proper, you did. . . . Well, I mus' be gettin' on. So long, young un. Remember me ter Robert."

He ambled down the path, out of the gate, down the road and disappeared from view.

William stood motionless, considering the situation
. . . and the warm glow of complacency that the man's
words had sent through his heart began to give way to
a slightly chilly feeling.   It was all right, of course.
Of *course*, it was all right.   The man had given Robert
the ten shillings and then collected the coat.   It *must*
be all right. . . .   He'd go to the old barn now, anyway.
He was late already.   He picked up his bow and arrow
and again stood motionless, his horrified eyes fixed
on the gate.   A small neat man in black jacket
striped trousers and bowler hat, was just coming in
He had a small neat face with small neat features and
he wore a small neat pair of spectacles.

"My name's Cooper," he said, in a quick, high-
pitched voice.   "I've come about that sports coat that
was advertised in the paper shop in Hadley by—your
brother, wasn't it?"

William's throat was dry.

"My—my brother's out," he said desperately.

"But I understood that he was leaving some message
about it," said Mr. Cooper irritably.   Mr. Cooper was
evidently a man who didn't like having his plans upset.
Certainly he was not a man to whom the true facts of
the case could be divulged with any hope of sympathy.

William stretched his lips in a ghastly smile of pro-
pitiation.

"I—I'm sorry, he's out.   He—he sort of said he'd
—he'd sort of got to be at cricket at two o'clock."

"If he left no proper message I won't waste any more
time on it," snapped Mr. Cooper.   "It's very annoy-
ing, but I'm going over to see some friends at Marleigh
and I'll call on my way back."

With that he turned on his heel and went briskly

out of the gate and down the road. His small neat figure vanished into the distance.

William stood staring after him blankly.

"Gosh!" he gasped, then, feeling the expression to be inadequate, added: "Crumbs!"

It was not the thought of Robert's reception of the news that filled him with horror (though the thought of that was enough to fill anyone with horror). It was the thought of having let Robert down, of having undertaken to do something for Robert and failed. . . . He decided that, at all costs, Robert's sports coat must be retrieved from its unlawful possessor before Mr. Cooper returned from Marleigh. And there was not a moment to be lost. He went to the gate and looked up and down the road. The road was empty in both directions. The tramp might have gone towards Hadley, towards Marleigh, across the fields, or through the woods. . . . William decided that it was not a job he could tackle alone and unaided. He must enlist the help of the Outlaws. . . .

Ginger, Henry and Douglas were at the door of the old barn waiting for him.

"Hello, William," said Ginger, mildly interested in William's meteoric arrival. "Is someone after you?"

"No," panted William, "but you've gotter help me catch a thief. He's stole Robert's sports coat—at least, he's same as stole it—an' we've gotter get it back before this Mr. Cooper comes. Listen . . ."

He told the story as quickly as he could.

"We've gotter spread out an' look for him," he said.

"We never have any luck with tramps," said Douglas. We didn't with that one of Archie's."

"Never mind that," interrupted William impatiently.

"He can't 've gone far. You go on the Hadley road, Douglas, an' Henry on the Marleigh road, an' Ginger 'n' me'll go to the village. We'll meet back here when we've finished searchin' an' I bet one of us'll have found it."

"S'pose he's desp'rate," said Douglas nervously. "Wish I'd got my water pistol."

"Shall I go home for our Father Christmas beard?" said Henry. "It's a jolly good disguise. He'd think I was an ole man an' let me get right up to him."

"*No*," said William firmly. "You've gotter be quick. Every minute he's gettin' further an' further away. We mustn't waste any more time."

The four set off at a brisk run. Douglas disappeared in the direction of Hadley, Henry in the direction of Marleigh, William and Ginger reached the outskirts of the village then slowed down to a walking pace.

"We've gotter search every inch," said William. "He might be in a hen-house or a greenhouse or anywhere, hidin' up till nightfall when he can escape with his loot."

"Thought you said it was a sports coat," said Ginger.

"I can't waste time teachin' you English," said William sternly. "Not now, when every minute's a matter of life and death. Come on. We've gotter search every *inch*."

The ensuing search resulted in their violent ejection from two back gardens, and a physical assault at the hands of an indignant householder, who discovered them in his shed turning over his store of carrots and onions.

"*And* you can think yourself lucky I've not handed you over to the police, you young rascals," he said, with a final cuff.

He was a stalwart householder and it was the cuff of an expert, depositing William neatly in the middle of the road.

"Gosh! I forgot he gave boxing lessons," said William, picking himself up and holding his head with both hands to make sure that it was still attached to his neck. "An' I like that! Callin' *us* thieves! Serve him right if the crim'nal *is* hid up among his carrots an' onions. It'd be a jolly good place to hide. All he'd gotter do was jus' to cover himself up with carrots an' onions an' no one'd think of lookin' under 'em. Like that man in the story of the barber and the forty thieves."

"Come on, William," said Ginger nervously. "He's watchin' us out of the window an' he's lookin' madder than ever."

"I'm not scared of him," said William, hurrying down the road as he spoke. He laughed shortly. "I bet he's scared of me, though. He went in jolly quick after he'd hit me, didn't he? He took jolly good care not to wait to be hit back, didn't he? *An'* he didn't come out again either. Huh! Serve him right if that ole tramp stole everythin' he'd got. An', if he does, he needn't come round to *me* for sympathy."

"I don't s'pose he would, anyway," said Ginger simply. "Well, the nex' house is Gen'ral Moult's. I don't s'pose he's hidin' there with the Gen'ral havin' 'Beware of the Dog' up."

"He's got no business to have that up when he hasn't got a dog," said William. "It's the same as tellin' a story."

"Well, he's got a cat with a jolly good scratch, 'cause we've tried it."

"Then he oughter have 'Beware of the Cat.' He—
Gosh! Look, Ginger."

The door of the garage was open and inside the
garage the General could be seen pottering about
among his rabbit hutches. But it was not the rabbits
or the rabbit hutches that made the eyes of William
and Ginger almost start out of their heads. It was
the brown check sports coat that hung loosely from the
General's shoulders.

"That's it!" gasped William excitedly. "Gosh!
That's Robert's sports coat. I'd know it anywhere."

"That man must've heard we were on his track,"
said Ginger, "an' he got scared an' sold it to the
Gen'ral or gave it him or somethin'."

"It may be worse than that," said William darkly.
"Gen'ral Moult may be the sort of head of a gang for
stealin' clothes. He may be in this crime wave what's
in the newspapers. Come to think of it, a man what
stops people goin' into fields for no reason at all—well,
he'd think nothin' of stealin' clothes. Anyway,
stoppin' people goin' into that field shows he's got
somethin' to hide. P'r'aps he's got boxes an' boxes
of black market sports coats an' things buried in it."

"I don't think so," said Ginger, whose imagination,
though lively enough, was incapable of the heights to
which William's could soar. "Not Gen'ral Moult."

"P'r'aps not," admitted William, coming down to
earth reluctantly. "Anyway, we've gotter get that
coat back. We'll jus' have to go an' tell him that it
was stole off Robert an' that he's gotter give it us
back."

They gazed uncertainly and a little apprehensively
at the figure of the General who, unconscious of their

presence, was distributing vegetables to his charges, barking out orders to them in his most military fashion.

"Come along, there, come along! Don't dawdle. Now, that's enough, you! Back to barracks with you. If you two are going to quarrel you shan't mess together in future. Quiet, there, quiet!"

"What are you goin' to say to him?" asked Ginger.

"Dunno yet," said William. "I'm thinkin'."

"You couldn't bring the Boer War into it, could you?" said Ginger. "He'd do anything for the Boer War."

"What d'you mean, he'd do anything for the Boer War?" said William irritably, but he knew quite well what Ginger meant. General Moult had fought in the Boer War as a young officer, and in his eyes it was the most outstanding event in the history of the world. He was aware that there had been two minor skirmishes since then, in which both his country and himself had played their parts, but nothing had yet happened, he considered, to equal the importance of the Relief of Mafeking or the Battle of Talana Hill. He was engaged in writing his memoirs, and had that morning written the greater part of the chapter on witch doctors. He stood now, a carrot in one hand and a brussels top in the other, his lips moving soundlessly as he went over the best bits of it.

Then two boys approached him. He knew them, of course. They were that couple of unruly young hooligans—William Brown and that friend of his—who had dared to make free with the field that was now his private property, rampaging about as if it belonged to them . . . shouting . . . climbing trees. Well, he had put a stop to that by writing very firmly to their fathers, and the matter should have been

D

finally settled. But here the boys were, coming, of course, to ask permission still to use the field in spite of his orders. The impudence and persistence of the modern boy, was, the General decided, beyond all bearing.

"Please, Gen'ral Moult——" began William.

"No, you shall *not*," said the General angrily. "I've written to your fathers and you must abide by what I've said. That field is my private property, and I will not have hooligans rampaging over it."

"Yes, but, Gen'ral Moult——" began Ginger.

Again the General interrupted him.

"What d'you think I bought it for?" he shouted. "D'you think I bought it for you to use as a playground? D'you think I went to all that trouble and expense just so that you could have somewhere to rampage and—and shout and—and climb trees and——"

The General was becoming almost inarticulate with rage.

"But we've come about the sports——" began William.

"*Sports!*" interrupted the General. "Call it sports indeed! Rampaging's what I call it. And, in any case, I did not buy that field to be used as a sports ground by all the boys in the village. I don't know how you dare to come to me after what I wrote to your fathers. The first time I catch either of you in that field I shall issue a summons for trespass. Sports indeed!"

Purple with fury, he advanced upon them, brandishing his carrot so threateningly that the two fled back to the road.

"Well, that wasn't much good," said Ginger.

"I bet he knew what we wanted really," said William. "He was tryin' to put us off the scent. Well, you could see he'd got a guilty conscience, carryin' on like that. He went all red an' hot same as people do with guilty consciences."

"I think that was 'cause he was so mad," said Ginger.

"He was pretendin' it was 'cause he was mad," said William, "but it was a guilty conscience really. I bet he knows he's got Robert's sports coat, an' I bet he's scared stiff now he knows we're on his track. Well, I'm not goin' back without it. Dunno why I didn't jus' take it off him. He couldn't've stopped me with that ole carrot. Look! He's goin' in now."

From under cover of the hedge they watched the General, still muttering angrily to himself, shut up the garage and return to the house.

"He's in his bedroom," said William. "I can see him movin' about. I bet he's goin' to write his book. He gen'rally writes his book in the afternoon. An' he wears that ole velvet jacket for writin' his book. . . . Yes, look. There he is!"

Through the hedge they could see General Moult entering his study, wearing the velvet jacket in which he always carried on his literary activities, and taking his place at the writing table near the window. The writing table was piled high with the forty diaries that the General had made during the Boer War. He had reached the five thousandth page of his manuscript and the third volume of the diary. As he said, the subject appeared to be inexhaustible. . . .

"He must've left Robert's sports coat in his bedroom," said William. "I'm goin' round to the side of the house an' I'm goin' to climb up that tree that you can see into his bedroom from, an' if it's there we've gotter get it."

"It's goin' to be jolly difficult," said Ginger, following William round to the side of the house, "an' I bet we'll both end up by bein' sent to prison."

"I wouldn't mind that," said William, as he swung himself up on to the lowest branch of the tree. "I've often thought I'd like to go to prison. You wouldn't have to go to school if you were in prison."

"They have rotten things to eat," said Ginger.

"They'd be a change from some of the things we have," said William, vanishing from sight into the leafy heights. "I say!"—his voice floated down— "I can see it. It's over the chair by his bed." He swarmed quickly down again, dropping from the lowest branch to join Ginger by the hedge. "We've gotter get it back. It's Robert's coat an' he's no right to keep it."

"We can't jus' take it," objected Ginger. "That'd be stealin'. P'r'aps he bought it. If he did, we oughter leave some money for it."

"We haven't got any money," said William simply.

"No, I know we've not. But we can't jus' go in an' take it."

"I s'pose we can't," agreed William reluctantly. "*Tell* you what! We can leave the value."

"What d'you mean, leave the value?" said Ginger.

"Well, s'pose he gave this tramp five shillin's for it—an' I bet he didn't give him more—we can leave five shillings' worth of things for him 'stead of the coat."

"We've not got five shillings' worth of things."

"I bet we have if we look round."

"He wouldn't want the sort of things we've got."

"I bet he would. He likes anythin' to do with South Africa an' I've got a Rhodesian stamp what my uncle sent me. I bet it's worth a lot of money. An' I say! What about your leopard claws off that rug what got the moth in. That came from South Africa, didn't it? An' I bet it was jolly valu'ble."

"Gosh! Yes, so it did," said Ginger.

For Ginger's mother had possessed a leopard skin rug into which the moth had made such inroads during the preceding summer that she had had to have it destroyed. Ginger had begged for the claws and they had been for some time his most valued possession.

"P'r'aps you don't want to give 'em up," said William, adding generously: "It doesn't matter if you don't want to. I bet we can find somethin' else."

"No, that's all right," said Ginger. "I'll give 'em up. I've shown 'em to everyone I know an' done all the things you can do with leopard claws. I don't want 'em any longer."

"Well, that's the stamp an' the leopard claws— I bet those leopard claws are jolly valu'ble—an' I'll fetch my penknife. A penknife's always useful, an' I've got two, 'cause Robert gave me another for my birthday. I bet that's about five shillings' worth. Can you think of anythin' else?"

"Gosh, yes, I can!" said Ginger. "It's Henry's, but I know where he keeps it an' he wouldn't mind us gettin' it. Don't you remember that wooden thing his uncle sent home? Jus' cut out of wood anyhow by natives in the shape of a sort of person with its eyes an' hair an' things done in what they call poker work. He sent it to Henry's sister really, but it made her cry, so they gave it to Henry, but Henry didn't want a rotten ole doll, so he jus' chucked it into his cupboard an' left it there."

"Yes, I remember. An' it came from South Africa, didn't it? Gosh! That's all right. That's four jolly valu'ble things. We'll go 'n' get 'em as quick as we can, an' we'll take the coat an' leave 'em there instead. We can get up into his bedroom easy by the tree, an' I know his ole housekeeper sleeps all afternoon. Come on. We've gotter be jolly quick. Let's run."

General Moult laid down his pen and leant back in his chair, frowning. He was feeling worried. He had finished the chapter on witch doctors, treating the subject lightly with a man-of-the-world amusement and incredulity. And he wasn't quite happy about it. Beneath his fire-eating exterior the General was a simple, credulous and rather timid man. He kept thinking about a witch doctor he had known in South Africa, who had escaped from any imprisonment however closely shackled and guarded. The General had become quite friendly with him, and they had had several long talks together.

"My magic is greater than time or space," the man had said. "However far you go from me, *baas*, I can always reach you if I want to."

Certainly some very peculiar things had happened to the witch doctor's enemies, however far they had gone from him. Sometimes he took some intimate personal possession of the enemy's and worked his magic through that. Sometimes he left a symbolic warning before he struck. Sometimes he struck without warning. Yes, some very peculiar and very unpleasant things had happened to people who

annoyed that witch doctor. The General's feeling of
nervousness increased. Perhaps it would be better
to treat the subject a little more seriously. The man,
if still alive, was a long way off, of course, but—one
never knew. The memory of the thin face and deep-
set eyes became strangely vivid, and he remembered
that nothing had so much annoyed the witch doctor
as any belittling of his magic powers. . . . He drummed
his fingers on the desk nervously. He was feeling
thoroughly put out. First those wretched boys coming
to pester him about the field in spite of the letters he
had written to their fathers, then this absurd nervousness about the witch doctor. It *was* absurd. He must
just try to conquer it. He would go upstairs and put
on his old gardening coat and, after ten minutes' dig-
ging in the open air, he would realise how childish
his fears had been.

He went upstairs, took off his velvet jacket, turned
to the chair by the bed, and stood transfixed by horror.
His well-worn gardening coat—his most intimate
personal possession—had vanished, and in its place
was a collection of objects that turned his blood to ice.
The roughly-carved wooden figure—obviously the work
of a native—bearing an uncanny likeness to the witch
doctor, the stamp of Rhodesia, where he had first
met the witch doctor, the leopard's claws and knife,
both suggesting unpleasant forms of death. He told
himself that such things didn't happen, and immediately
afterwards told himself again that they did. He came
to a sudden decision. The warning must be heeded,
the curse averted while there was yet time. He went
downstairs, took up his witch doctor chapter, tore
it across with trembling fingers and thrust it into the

WILLIAM WALKED BEHIND THE THREE STRANGE
FIGURES, WATCHING THEM WITH A DOUBTFUL FROWN.

waste paper basket.   Then he stood, considering. . . .
Was there any other means by which he could avert
the threatened doom?   He remembered his last
conversation with the witch doctor.   The old chap
had had a bee in his bonnet about land.   It should
not be enclosed, he had said in his shrill staccato
voice.   Every man, woman and child should have
free access to the land.   Evil would come to the man
who enclosed it and shut his fellow creatures out of it.
Perhaps—it seemed fantastic, but perhaps . . .   Better
be on the safe side.   The General sat down at his table
and wrote a letter to the father of each of the Outlaws,
saying that he had reconsidered his decision and that
the boys might continue to use his field on condition
that they did no damage.

He stamped the letters and took them out to the
post.   As he dropped them into the pillar-box he had
a curious feeling as if the curse were being lifted from
him. . . .

William and Ginger reached the old barn, carrying
the brown check sports coat.   Henry was its only
occupant.

"We've got it," said William triumphantly.   "Ole
Gen'ral Moult had it an' we bought it back off him.
At least, we sort of bought it back."

Then they stood staring at Henry in amazement,
for Henry, too, held a brown check sports coat.

"But *I* got it," said Henry.   "I jus' looked in at the
Village Hall an' there it was on Miss Milton's jumble
stall.   I thought he'd guessed we were after him an'
took fright an' slipped it on the stall, so I—so I jus'
slipped it off again."

"Crumbs!" gasped Ginger, "but there can't be two of them."

At this point Douglas arrived.   He carried a brown check sports coat.

"I've got it," he said triumphantly.   "It was on Farmer Jenks's scarecrow in Three Acre Meadow."

Then he saw the others and his jaw dropped open.

"Gosh!" he stammered.   "There can't be *three* of 'em."

William collected his scattered forces with difficulty.

"Well, one of 'em mus' be Robert's," he said, "an' we've gotter find out which. . . . Come on.   Let's take 'em home an' see."

They set off down the road, Ginger, Henry and Douglas each carrying a brown check sports coat over his arm.

"I votes we put 'em on an' wear 'em," said Ginger. "It'll look more nat'ral than carryin' 'em like this."

Pleased with the suggestion, they put them on and wore them.   The ends of the coats reached their knees.   The shoulders dangled almost to their elbows. William walked behind the three strange figures, watching them with a doubtful frown.

"It does look more nat'ral, doesn't it?" asked Ginger anxiously.

"Well," said William, "I dunno that I'd call it *nat'ral* but, anyway, it doesn't matter.   We're nearly home now."

They reached the gate of William's house and stood there uncertainly.

"I b'lieve Robert's back," said William, looking up at the window of Robert's bedroom.   "Yes, I can see him brushin' his hair.   You stay behind the hedge where he can't see you an' I'll try 'n' find out which *is* his coat."

The three small figures, each swamped in its brown check sports coat, withdrew into the shadow of the hedge.

"I bet it's mine," said Henry. "I took an awful lot of trouble gettin' it off ole Miss Milton's stall."

"I bet it's mine," said Douglas. "It took a bit of nerve, I can tell you, takin' it off that scarecrow right in the middle of the field."

"Huh!" snorted Ginger. "William an' me went into the very jaws of death for ours. I bet ole Gen'ral Moult 'd've murdered us if he'd come in an' found us."

William entered the house and stood for a moment in the hall. The door of Robert's bedroom opened and Robert appeared. He descended the stairs slowly, fixing William with a stern accusing gaze.

"I say, Robert," began William nervously, "about that sports coat."

"Yes, a nice mess you made of it, didn't you?" said Robert.

"But, you see, Robert——" began William, playing for time. Robert interrupted him.

"Why on earth didn't you give it to the man when he came?"

William moistened his lips.

"Well, you see, Robert," he said. "It was this way, Robert. You see, this other man——"

"What other man?" snapped Robert. "I don't know what you're talking about. What I want to know is, why didn't you give Mr. Cooper the coat when he called for it?"

"I've got it now," said William. "Well, as a matter

of fact, I've got three of 'em now.   You can choose one an' we'll take the others back."

Robert stared at him helplessly.

"I haven't the faintest idea what you're talking about," he said.   "Mr. Cooper called back for the coat after he'd been to Marleigh, and I gave it him and got his ten bob.   I might have missed it altogether with you playing the fool like that."

William's mouth opened and shut like the mouth of an expiring fish.   It was some moments before he found his voice.

"You—you gave it him?" he gasped.

"Of course I did."

"But—but where did you find it, Robert?"

"Find it?   In my wardrobe, of course, where it's always been."

"N—n—n—not in the tool shed?"

"Tool shed?   Of course not."

"But—but there *was* one in the tool shed," said William desperately.

"Oh, that old thing," said Robert.   "I thought mother had sent that to a jumble sale months ago. I'd said she could."

"Oh," said William blankly.

"And you darn well won't get that sixpence now. Messing things up like that!"

"No, Robert," agreed William dazedly.

Dazedly he went out to join the strange group by the gate, huddled together in brown check sports coats.

"I say," he whispered.   "We've gotter get 'em back, all of 'em, quick.   None of 'em's Robert's.   Come on, Ginger.   We'll go back to Gen'ral Moult's, an' you, Henry, go back to——"

He looked down the road and his voice trailed away into silence. General Moult was approaching and even from the distance it was plain that he was a very angry man. Behind him walked Miss Milton, indignation in every line of her thin angular figure. He looked up the road. From that direction Farmer Jenks was bearing down on them, his face purple, his arms swinging aggressively. The Outlaws realised with sinking hearts that their depredations had not been without witnesses and that the witnesses had taken the first convenient opportunity of informing the owners of the exact circumstances in which their property had disappeared. All three had traced the "thefts" to William's house and were out for vengeance and their sports coats. General Moult was the angriest of them all because he could not bring himself to cancel the permission to use his field that he had just posted to the Outlaws' fathers. (You never know, he couldn't help thinking. There might be something in it . . . Better be on the safe side.) But he meant to take it out of those young rascals, none the less.

Helplessly the group by William's gate awaited its fate, shrinking so far into its sports coats that nothing seemed to be left of it but expanses of brown check.

"Gosh!" groaned William. "Fancy there bein' four of them!"

But he had forgotten.

There were five.

At that moment the tramp who was the original cause of all the trouble was curled up on a comfortable bed of bracken in a sheltered corner of the wood, snug in Robert's old sports coat, deep in a dreamless sleep.

CHAPTER IV

A WITCH IN TIME

WILLIAM read the letter several times with frowning concentration.

"DEAR WILLIAM,

"We can't come home because we let it to Miss Evesham unfurnished and we can't get her out and Mummy and I want to come home and do you remember when we were turned out because of that bomb you got us back and *please*, William, will you get us back again because Mummy and I are both so homesick and you're so clever I know you can.

"Love from
"JOAN."

His feeling of importance at receiving a letter (for his correspondence was a very limited one) was mingled with a feeling of uneasiness. He had heard his parents discussing the situation. He knew that Joan's mother had employed a solicitor to try to evict Miss Evesham and that the whole power of the law had been unable to accomplish it. Miss Evesham clung grimly to her rights, and to Joan's home, refusing all "alternative accommodation."

In face of this, William found Joan's faith in him touching but a little embarrassing. True, he had been

the instrument of Fate in restoring their home to her
and her mother on the occasion when they had been
ejected for a supposed "delayed action bomb," but
this was a very different matter. Difficulty, however,
was always a challenge to William, and—he wanted
Joan back. He liked Joan. She was quiet and shy,
and amenable and dependable, and he was a god in her
eyes. The last alone would have endeared her to
William, who was a god in very few people's eyes. He
had never failed her yet, and to fail in this task she so
disconcertingly thrust upon him might be to lose her
admiration for ever. But he thought of the hatchet-
faced, keen-eyed, slit-mouthed solicitor who had
visited Miss Evesham in a final effort to eject her and
had retired completely routed. How should he,
William, succeed where such a man had failed?

And yet—it would be nice to have Joan and her
mother back in place of the obnoxious Miss Evesham.
For Miss Evesham *was* obnoxious. Even Mrs. Brown,
notoriously charitable in her judgments, said that she
was the most disagreeable woman she had ever met.
And her cat, Hector, was, if possible, more unpleasant
even than his mistress. He was a black cat with a
white muzzle and a villainous expression. He came
through the hedge into the Browns' garden and lay
in wait for their birds. Mr. Brown was a bird lover.
He had a bird bath and a bird table and a tame robin
and chaffinch. Or rather he had the last two before
Hector's arrival. Hector made short work of them,
and of the other birds who had come to regard the
Browns' garden as a sanctuary.

Mr. Brown wrote an angry letter to Miss Evesham.
Miss Evesham replied by informing Mr. Brown that

to eat birds was a cat's instinct and that she had always encouraged Hector to follow his instincts. She added to this a page of complaints about William, whom she accused of taking short cuts through her garden to the detriment of both lawn and flower beds, of making her head ache with his mouth organ, and of taking pot-shots at Hector through the bathroom window.

Mr. Brown sternly warned William against any further hostilities.

"She's an odious woman and he's an odious cat," he said, "but we put ourselves entirely in the wrong by that sort of thing. You can chase the creature out of the garden if it comes in, but otherwise you'll leave it alone or you'll have me to deal with."

Since then, William had confined himself to "chasing the creature out of the garden" in as many ways as he could devise, and pulling faces at it over the fence. He had known cats who could be driven to frenzy by this last treatment, but Hector merely gazed back at him with sleepy green eyes.

William read the letter again. He would have to think out a plan, but it wouldn't be easy. . . . And there wasn't time even to start thinking it out to-day, because to-day was the day on which his air-gun was being restored to him by his father after one of its recurrent periods of retirement. The occasion of its retirement had been the breaking of a pane of glass in Miss Milton's greenhouse, and his father had been grimmer than usual over it.

"The next time anything of this sort happens, my boy," he had said, "you can say good-bye to it for good. I'm getting tired of these complaints."

To-day Ginger was going to call for him, and the

two were taking the newly restored air-gun out for a morning's exercise.

"It's jolly mean of him to keep taking it away like this," said William. "I get all out of practice. Serve him right if we lose the nex' war with me not bein' able to shoot straight. Let's go'n' practice in your garden."

They practised in Ginger's garden, but neither Ginger nor William seemed able to hit anything they aimed at. Bottles remained unbroken, tins undented.

"It's all *his* fault," said William gloomily. "He mus' have messed it up somehow. Jus' chucked it down anywhere, I 'spect, an' got somethin' bent inside it. . . . Well, it mus' be that 'cause it always hits somethin' I'm not aimin' at. Hits somethin' about six inches away. Stands to reason he's got it bent somewhere."

It was now lunch time, so the two decided to meet again in the afternoon and work on that theory.

"I bet we find that's it," said William. "If we want to hit anythin' we've got to aim about six inches to the side of it."

The church clock struck one as William sauntered homewards, his air-gun under his arm.

"Gosh, I'd better hurry," he thought.

He was passing Miss Evesham's garden. The short cut—through a hole in Miss Evesham's hedge, across her garden and over the fence—would save time, and he decided to risk it. Miss Evesham, he knew, was not at home. He had seen her waiting at the bus stop to go into Hadley. He scrambled through the hole and began to walk over the lawn. Well, he

justified himself, she can't say I'm doin' any harm.
What's grass for but to be walked on?

Suddenly he saw Hector crouching by the edge of
the lawn, watching him with a sardonic leer. About
six inches away from him was a rose pole.

I bet, if I aimed at that cat, I'd hit the rose pole,
thought William. Couldn't do it any harm. It
looks a jolly strong rose pole.

He took careful aim at Hector and fired. . . .

After his chastening experiences of the morning he
was prepared to miss the rose pole. What he was not
prepared for was to see Hector leap two feet into the
air, descend to the earth and lie still.

"*Gosh!*" said William, aghast.

Trembling with apprehension, he approached his
old foe and examined him. There was no doubt of it.
Hector's troubles were over. William's, it seemed,
were just beginning. . . .

The first thing to do, of course, was to dispose of the
body. William looked round guiltily. There seemed
to be no witnesses of the crime. Bundling Hector
under his coat, he scrambled over the fence, concealed
Hector in the pile of leaf mould at the bottom of the
garden, and went indoors to lunch.

"You look rather pale, dear," said Mrs. Brown
solicitously. "Do you feel quite well?"

William assured her that he felt quite well and, in
spite of the weight on his mind, proceeded to prove it
by disposing of three large helpings of shepherd's pie
and three large baked apples with custard.

"Did you have a good morning's sport with your
gun?" said Mrs. Brown cheerfully.

William gave a bitter laugh.

"Oh, yes . . . a jolly good morning's sport!" he said.

Immediately after lunch he made his way down to the heap of leaf mould and disinterred Hector. Impossible, of course, to leave him there. If he did, the gardener would be certain to start burrowing in the heap first thing to-morrow morning. Impossible for the same reason to bury him anywhere in the garden. With the perversity of Fate, that would be the exact spot out of the whole garden that the gardener would choose to dig over the next time he came. Jenks's pond in Three Acre Meadow was the best solution, but there were drawbacks even to that. It was in full view of the road, and anyone passing and seeing William engaged in his sinister task would remember the fact and later connect it with the disappearance of Hector. Miss Evesham herself even might chance to be passing on a bus. . . . Still, the risk must be taken, so William picked up Hector, bundled him again under his coat, and set off for the pond. Even his passage along the road was fraught with danger. Hector was a big cat and William, though strong and healthy, was not a big boy. Any officious neighbour, meeting him, might demand to know the nature of the strange excrescence beneath his coat.

He was relieved to see that the road was empty except for a boy about his own age coming from the opposite direction, carrying a basket covered with sacking. Even he, however, gave proof of the curiosity that the contours of William's torso were likely to excite. He stopped.

"What've you got under your coat?" he demanded.

"What've you got in your basket?" countered William, scowling aggressively.

"A cat," said the boy.

"Oh," said William, taken aback.

"A cat, an' I'm sick of it," added the boy with feeling. "It's as heavy as lead an' it keeps tryin' to get out. . . . What is it under your coat?"

"A cat, too, an' I'm sick of it, too," said William.

"Where are you takin' it?"

"To the pond. Where are you takin' yours?"

"To the vet. to be put to sleep. It's ole Miss Peter's an' she's let Honeysuckle Cottage to someone an' she's goin' up North an' she doesn't want to take the cat with her, an' she doesn't think he'd be happy with this person that's comin' to Honeysuckle Cottage an' he's gettin' old, anyway, so she's havin' him put to sleep. An' she's only givin' me sixpence. Gosh! I'm wore out with it already."

"Let's have a look at it."

Cautiously the boy removed the sacking. William gasped. It was a black cat with a white muzzle— the spit and image of Hector.

"I say!" he said excitedly. "Will you swop?"

"How d'you mean, swop?" said the boy suspiciously.

"Well, mine's dead. It'll save you goin' to the vet."

"Yes, but I've got to take it on to the taxi person in Hadley afterwards. He's goin' to stuff it for her. She says it's been her only friend for five long years an' she wants to have its dear face to look at."

"Gosh! She mus' be bats."

"I'll say she is! I'd had enough of its dear face, *an'* its dear claws, in five long minutes."

"What's its name?"

"Lucifer. Lucy for short. . . . I say, what are you carryin' a dead cat about for?"

"OH, WILLIAM, HOW GOOD OF YOU!" EXCLAIMED
MISS EVESHAM.

"Never mind that," said William. "Look here, if we swop, you needn't bother to go to the vet. at all. You can jus' take my cat straight to that man in Hadley to be stuffed. It'll save you a lot of trouble. An' they're just alike. She'll never know."

"Gosh! They *are* alike, aren't they?"

"Yes, an' you won't have any trouble with this one. He was somethin' awful when he was alive, but he's all right now."

"Very well," said the boy, after a moment's hesitation. "It's her own fault, only givin' me sixpence, but ——"

Quickly, without giving him time to reconsider the matter, William snatched Lucifer from the basket, bundled Hector into it, and with a "Cheerio" set off briskly down the road.

"Here! I say!" called the boy, but William, pretending not to hear, climbed the stile into the field and disappeared.

Lucifer was inclined to resent this sudden change, but William pinioned him firmly under his coat and carried him towards his new home. As he neared the new home he slackened his pace somewhat and began to wonder how to introduce him into it. If he just put him down in the garden he would probably make off at once to his old home. The best thing would be to slip him through a window, close the window and leave him to it. But as he approached the house the front door opened and, to his dismay, Miss Evesham came out. She looked pale and anxious.

"William," she said. "I can't think what's happened to Hector. Have you seen him anywhere?"

William opened his coat and brought out Lucifer.

"I saw him on the road an' brought him along," he said, with a glow of virtue at the thought that he was only speaking the exact truth.

"Oh, William," said Miss Evesham, deeply touched by this unexpected kindness. "That was very good of you. Bring him in. . . . Poor old Hector! Why did you run away, my precious? He's in a very nervous state, isn't he? I hope he's not been run over or anything."

"I think he's all right," said William.

Miss Evesham was anxiously feeling Lucifer's joints.

"Yes, he seems all right. . . . He must just have had a fright. Perhaps some horrible dog chased him, or perhaps he was nearly run over. . . . Here's your tea, Hector darling."

Lucifer suddenly espied the two saucers on which his "tea" was spread—top of the milk bottle on one and four sardines in the other—and his nervousness perceptibly diminished. He set to work at once, crouching over the saucers and only stopping occasionally to purr. Miss Evesham watched him fondly.

"You're all right now, aren't you, darling!" she said.

Evidently he was. Gorged with cream and sardines, he staggered to the nearest chair, flopped down into it, and went sound asleep.

"*That's* my Hector," said Miss Evesham, little knowing how far from the truth this simple statement was.

William crept quietly away.

That should have been the end of it, but it wasn't.

The next afternoon, Miss Evesham's face, wearing a woebegone expression, appeared suddenly over the fence.

"William," she said, "he's gone again."

William was annoyed. He was trying to think out a plan for ejecting Miss Evesham from her house, and he didn't want to be interrupted.

"Has he?" he said coldly.

"Yes. I want you to take me to the place where you found him before."

"It was jus' on the road. I told you," said William.

"But, William, please come with me and show me exactly."

The sight of Miss Evesham, humble and suppliant, went to William's head. Never before had that face appeared over the fence except in frowning displeasure.

"All right," he said, with the air of one reluctantly conceding a favour. "I'll come."

He led her across the field to the point in the road where he had met the boy with the basket.

"I met him jus' here," he said.

"Coming from that direction?" said Miss Evesham.

"Yes," said William.

"Let's go along the road a little further," said Miss Evesham. "We may find him. . . ."

And they found him. . . .

He was sitting on the doorstep of Honeysuckle Cottage, calmly washing his face. On seeing them he stood up and went indoors, tail erect.

Miss Evesham hovered irresolute in the open doorway.

"Hector!" she called pleadingly, in an undertone.

There was no answer.

Miss Evesham knocked at the door.

An old lady came to the door. She had white hair, a nut-cracker nose and mouth and she walked with a stick. In spite of all this, she looked quite a pleasant old lady.

Miss Evesham fixed her with a stern accusing eye.

"I've come for my cat," she said.

"Oh, your cat," said the old lady. She looked over her shoulder. "Is he your cat? I didn't know whose he was. He comes and goes. I give him milk when I have any. I'm not really a cat lover. Come in, won't you?"

They followed her into the little sitting-room, where Lucifer was curled up in a chair by the fire. On the table was a typewriter and a jumble of manuscript.

"My name's Miss Perrott," said the old lady, "and I've come here to do a little writing in peace and quiet. I'm afraid the cottage is damp, though, because my rheumatism is much worse since I came here."

"My name's Miss Evesham," said Miss Evesham, unsmiling. "And I'll take my cat now if I may."

"Certainly, certainly," said Miss Perrott, seating herself at the table in front of the typewriter. She smiled faintly as Miss Evesham approached Lucifer. "He doesn't seem to know you very well, does he?"

Miss Evesham looked at her darkly.

"He did before he came here."

The old lady smiled again.

"Really?" she said.

Miss Evesham set off for home with Lucifer in her arms and a deep frown on her brow.

"I didn't like her," she said to William, "not from the minute she answered the door, I didn't. She'd got witch written all over her."

"There aren't any witches nowadays," said William.

Miss Evesham gave a snort.

"People *think* there aren't," she said, "but it's a subject I happen to be interested in. I read a book on witches just before I came here, *proving* that they're still about and just as powerful as they ever were. And a sister of mine once stayed in a village in Cornwall, where there was a woman who could ill-wish anyone she liked. . . . Didn't you *smell* evil in the atmosphere as soon as she came to the door?"

William said that he thought he'd smelt ginger-bread but that was all.

"And what's she doing *luring* my cat from me?" continued Miss Evesham earnestly. "That's where he must have been that first afternoon when you found him. Never wandered before in all his life, and then suddenly starts going to *her* cottage. He'd never go of his own accord. She must have put a spell on him."

"Why should she?" demanded William.

"They've got to have cats, haven't they?" said Miss Evesham. "Perhaps she couldn't bring hers, and that's why she's trying to get mine. Perhaps they have to be black with just that white spot. I don't know. . . . But she shan't have my Hector . . . I'll save you from her, my precious."

Her precious, confronted again with cream and sardines, ate with every appearance of enjoyment and again went to sleep on the chair.

His mistress watched him with anxious affection.

William returned slowly and thoughtfully to his own garden. He had discovered the weak spot in his enemy's armour. He must now try to devise some way of using it. . . .

.   .   .   .   .

As far as the Browns were concerned, Lucifer was an improvement on Hector. He did not trespass in their garden and he had no taste for birds. He divided his time between his old home and his new—drawn to the old by the force of association, and to the new by top-of-the-bottle and sardines. Miss Evesham seemed to have quite forgotten her feud with William and regarded him as her friend and ally.

"William," she said one morning, meeting him in the village, "he's gone off to that witch again."

"I don't think she's a witch," said William mildly.

"How does she manage to lure him to her cottage like that if she's not put a spell on him? He goes as if something *drew* him there. And it's not only that. His whole nature's changed. He's not the same cat as he was before she put this spell on him. Everything about him's different. His ways are different. Even his purr seems to have a different note. And he's lost all his affection for me."

"It'll come back," William assured her.

"It's not so much the *cat*, William," said Miss Evesham, lowering her voice, "as what it stands for. I've always been interested in the subject, as I told you, and I've read a lot about it. I know that witchcraft still goes on—chiefly in small, out-of-the-way villages like this. Casual visitors, of course, never see it. It goes on *beneath* the surface of normal uneventful village life. I read a story once about a village like this—quite an ordinary village on the surface and, in the day time, everyone peacefully pursuing their occupation, but at night the whole village would meet secretly and indulge in *orgies* of witchcraft. I haven't a suspicious nature, William, but if everything is as it seems to be in this village, why is that woman here, and why is she putting a spell on my cat? There's some reason behind it."

William saw a dim light very far ahead. It wasn't bright enough to be called an idea, but it might lead to one. . . .

"It's funny you should say that," he said slowly.

"What, William?"

"About the village and—witchcraft and that sort of thing. Lots of things have been happening here that I couldn't quite understand."

"What sort of things?" said Miss Evesham eagerly.

"I don't think I'd better talk about them," said William, giving a convincing performance of nervousness. "I—might get into trouble."

"Oh, but you can to *me*, William. I won't tell a soul. I'll do my best to put a stop to it, but I won't betray you."

"Well," said William, as if the confidence were being dragged out of him against his will, "There *have* been some funny goings-on here. Meetin's and things in the Village Hall after dark. Everyone went to them. They were supposed to be jus' ordinary meetin's with speakers, but—well, there was somethin' funny about them an' I've often wondered what really happened at them."

"Did your father and mother go to them?"

"Oh, yes . . . after I was in bed. I once got up to look out of the window, an' it was moonlight, an' the road was full of people goin' to one of these meetin's an' they all had a—funny sort of look."

Miss Evesham shuddered.

"How horrible! That's just as it was described in

this story I told you of. . . . Something must be *done*, you know. I don't suppose you realise that these orgies sometimes entail human sacrifice?"

"Y—yes," admitted William, "an' people *have* disappeared. Not people who live here, but people who were jus' stayin' here."

He looked at her hopefully, but evidently the hint of this danger was not sufficient to make Miss Evesham vacate the commodious premises in which she was now so snugly ensconced.

"It's too terrible to think of," she said. "Now, William, I want you to help me. You're only a child, but I see that you're not yet tainted by the poison. I want you to report to me anything suspicious you may see or hear. I realise, of course, that I run a certain risk by staying here at the heart of this evil and working against it, but I was never one to be turned from duty by danger."

"Well, there's one other thing," said William, with a burst of inspiration. "My father's got a book with *Laws of Banking* on the outside, but I think there's something quite different inside. Once I got hold of it an' he shouted 'Leave that alone'."

"Can you get the book, William, and bring it to me?"

"'Fraid I can't. He'd miss it at once an' he's a very savage man."

"I'm sure he is. This sort of thing has a very brutalising effect on the character. . . . But perhaps you could just peep into it when no one's looking and tell me what you see."

Fate seemed to be on William's side, for the next time that Miss Evesham went in search of the errant Lucifer it happened to be a very misty morning, and it happened, too, that Miss Perrott was having her chimney swept. Through the mist, Miss Evesham just saw the end of a brush vanishing down the chimney. She turned pale and fled back to the shelter of her own home. Lucifer's arrival a few minutes later, his coat bearing distinct traces of soot, confirmed her worst suspicions. . . .

"People laugh at these old ideas of the witch flying through the air on her broomstick," she said to William, "but they're not invented. They're traditions, handed down from the days when such things were openly done and accepted. Now they are only done in secret, but the—the *ritual* is the same. . . . Have you been able to look at that book of your father's yet, William?"

"Not yet," said William.

He was feeling a little troubled. His plan had seemed at first a brilliant one, but it was defeating its own ends. Instead of frightening Miss Evesham away from the neighbourhood, it was making her more determined than ever to stay and investigate the mare's nest which he had been at such pains to provide for her.

He was frequently sent to Honeysuckle Cottage to bring back the errant Lucifer, and had struck up a friendship with Miss Perrott. He liked her. She was vague and friendly and inconsequent, gave him any sweets or biscuits she happened to have, and encouraged him to talk to her. Visiting her one afternoon, he was considerably startled to find the stuffed figure of Hector standing in a life-like attitude on her table.

"The wretched owner of the cottage has sent it down," she explained. "It evidently belonged to her

and died, and she's had it stuffed and asks me to keep
it safe for her here as she's paying a series of visits
and it's an awkward thing to travel about with. I'm
sure it is. . . . It's not unlike that horrible cat that
keeps coming here, is it? But all cats are the same.
I dislike them intensely. They're so feline, though I
suppose one can't justly blame them for that. I'll
put the ghastly thing away somewhere where I can't
see it." She bundled Hector unceremoniously into a
large cupboard and closed the door. "Now, William,
I wonder if you'd do something for me. I want to get
up an Anti-Vivisection meeting while I'm here. I'm
not keen on Causes on the whole, but I really have that
very much at heart. No one seems to have done anything to rouse interest in it here, so I thought I'd start
the good work. . . . Do people come to meetings
here?"

"Oh, yes," said William. "They like 'em. There's
nothin' much else to do."

"Well, then, if I type the notices, will you take them
round for me? I'd be most grateful if you would."

William agreed and went home thoughtfully. He
felt that this should be his opportunity of speeding up
the plan that was so lamentably hanging fire, if only
he could see how to do it. . . . He put in a bit of spade-
work by calling on Miss Evesham and saying, in the
conspiratorial whisper they used in discussing the
question: "I've found out what Hector's witch-name
is."

"Witch-name?" said Miss Evesham perplexed.

"Yes. They give 'em a different name when they've
taught them to do witch work. They call Hector
Lucifer."

Miss Evesham paled and looked at the lawn where Lucifer lay enjoying the sunshine.

"Call him by it an' see what he does," suggested William.

"L—l—lucifer," called Miss Evesham nervously.

Lucifer sprang up and ran to her, rubbing himself against her legs.

"Oh, my poor Hector!" she moaned. "What *have* they done to you?"

All this, however, didn't seem to be getting William any nearer his aim, which was the removal of Miss Evesham from the house she so wrongfully occupied. He couldn't blame Miss Evesham herself. She was so credulous as to make the whole thing child's play. But he didn't seem able to lead her credulity in the right direction. . . .

She was full of excitement when she received the notice of the meeting on Anti-Vivisection.

"It's one of those meetings you told me of, William," she said. "Got up by that woman, too. That in itself would be proof, if proof were needed. I shall certainly go and see with my own eyes what happens. Do try and look at that book of your father's before the meeting. I believe that each centre has its own ritual, handed down through the generations and, of course, they all differ in detail."

A gleam came into William's eyes. Faintly in the distance he saw his nebulous plan taking more definite shape.

The next day he paid three calls.

First he went to Miss Perrott's.

"Why don't you have that stuffed cat on the table for your meeting?" he said. "I bet people would like it."

E

"That's quite an idea," said Miss Perrott. "'I love little pussy,' you mean. Yes, it might touch some heart's chord. It's worth trying."

"I'll carry it down for you," offered William.

"Thank you. That would be a help. I have so many papers and things, and my rheumatism isn't getting any better."

"An'—there's one other thing. You know Miss Evesham?"

"That stupid woman who comes here for her cat? Yes."

"Well, I think she'd give you a lot of money for the Society in Aid of Vivisection."

"Anti-Vivisection, William dear."

"Yes, that. But she likes to be important. She'd like to be on the platform."

"Well, there's no reason why she shouldn't be. I'll send her a note."

"N—no, not that way," said William slowly. "She was tellin' me about a meetin' she'd been to, an', when everyone was there an' the meetin' was jus' goin' to begin, the person on the platform saw her down in the audience an' called her up to the platform an' she liked it, 'cause everyone heard it an' watched her goin' up to the platform. It made her feel sort of important. She gave 'em quite a lot of money."

Miss Perrott smiled—a smile in which pity and contempt were mingled.

"I know the mentality only too well. But I do need money for the funds, so I'll pander to it."

"You'll call her up to the platform jus' before this meetin' in aid of Vivisection begins?"

"Anti-Vivisection, dear. Yes, I certainly will."

So far, so good, thought William. But there was still a lot to be done.

He next approached Mr. Westonbury.

Mr. Westonbury was the self-appointed Master of Ceremonies of any function in which he found himself. He fussed about and opened windows and closed doors, or closed windows and opened doors, and gave directions to everyone whether he knew what they ought to be doing or not. He was a sidesman in church and showed every member of the congregation to his seat, though there was no need to do it as the same people had sat in the same seats ever since anyone could remember. At concerts he "gave out" the items, at dances he "gave out" the dances, at plays he "gave out" the *dramatis personæ* and scenes. It was torture to him to have no official part in any proceeding. If he hadn't one, he pretended to have one. If he could do nothing else, he stood up in the front of the hall and looked important. He was a tall, thick-set man with beetling eyebrows, a tense expression, and a habit of saying: "Yes, yes, yes."

"Mr. Westonbury," said William, accosting him the next morning in the village.

"Yes, yes, yes," said Mr. Westonbury, as if he could hardly spare the time to say it.

"You know Miss Evesham, what's come to live nex' door to us?"

"Yes, yes, yes," said Mr. Westonbury.

"An' you know Miss Perrott what's gettin' up this meetin' in aid of Vivisection?"

"Anti, my boy, anti. Yes, yes, yes."

"Well, I think Miss Perrott's goin' to ask Miss Evesham to go up to the platform an' if she does Miss

Evesham *wants* to go up to the platform, but she doesn't think she can manage the steps. They're a bit steep, you know, an' she's afraid of fallin'; so would you help her up them to the platform?"

"Yes, yes, yes," said Mr. Westonbury, brightening perceptibly.

"But don't say anythin' to her about it if you see her. She's a bit shy about it, an', of course, Miss Perrott may not ask her up, but if she does she'd be very glad if you'd help her up them. She asked me to ask you an' to ask you not to say anythin' to her about it, 'cause she feels a bit shy about it. . . ."

"Yes, yes, yes," said Mr. Westonbury, squaring his shoulders and bending his arms as if to encircle Miss Evesham's far from faëry form. "Delighted, of course. I quite understand. Yes, yes, yes."

And he went on his way, his grim face relaxed almost to a smile. . . . For that evening, at any rate, he was saved from obscurity.

There was still Miss Evesham to be tackled—the most tricky part of the whole thing. William had the wisdom to wait till she tackled him, and to appear to be reluctant to give his information. She lay in wait for him the next afternoon and tackled him as soon as he reached the road.

"William," she said, "have you looked at that book of your father's yet?"

"Well, yes," said William. "An' it is about witchcraft, but I couldn't understand it. I don't think it would int'rest you."

"It *would*, William," said Miss Evesham. "You must tell me every *word*. It's most important, with this meeting coming on."

"WILL YOU COME UP ON TO THE PLATFORM, MISS
EVESHAM?" SHE SAID. THE BLOOD FROZE IN MISS
EVESHAM'S VEINS.

"Well, you know . . . about those meetin's an' how they could pretend they were about things like Vivisection so as not to arouse suspicion in outsiders, an'—but it sounds so silly," he ended.

"William, you must tell me *everything*," persisted Miss Evesham.

"Well," continued William, "It seemed to be somethin' about a sort of wooden altar with a hypnotised cat on it."

"A *what?*"

"A hypnotised cat."

"How extraordinary!"

"That's what I thought," said William. "That's why I thought it was too silly to tell you."

"What else did it say?" asked Miss Evesham excitedly. "Did it say anything about human sacrifice?"

"Y—yes," said William. "It seemed to be somethin' about a—a priestess standin' behind this wooden altar with this hypnotised cat on it, an' that the human sacrifice mus' be the person this cat belongs to, an'—then I heard my father comin' an' had to put the book back."

"I shall be there," said Miss Evesham firmly. "I shall sit right in the front so that I can see *everything* that happens. I shall watch so carefully that nothing can escape me, and then, even at the peril of my life, I shall expose the whole diabolical business."

As the day of the meeting drew near, William became more and more anxious. His calculations depended largely on chance, and chance, as he had learnt by experience, was not always to be depended on.

The village turned out in force for the meeting, less owing to any strong local interest in Anti-Vivisection than to a dearth of rival attractions.

Miss Evesham entered the hall, wearing a grim set look, casting challenging glances at the faces around her. Most of the faces wore a bored expression for, though their owners had come for want of something better to do, they cherished no great hopes of the evening. How *satanic* they all look, thought Miss Evesham, with a shudder, as she made her way to the front row. . . .

The curtains dividing the platform from the hall were drawn, for no other reason than that Mr. Westonbury enjoyed drawing them back. The clock struck eight and Mr. Westonbury, with his own inimitable air of providing the most important item of the evening's entertainment, drew them back.

Miss Evesham gave a gasp of horror. For there on the platform was the wooden table (the altar, she supposed) and on it was Hector . . . *her* Hector, whom she had left asleep by the fire, now spirited here by some infernal means and standing motionless, not moving a muscle or twitching a whisker . . . *hypnotised* . . .

And behind the altar was Miss Perrott, looking more witch-like than ever—hatless, her white hair falling about her face, wearing a long black coat and leaning on a stick.

Then came the culmination of the horror.

For the witch hobbled to the edge of the platform, looked down into the well of the hall, fixed her gimlet eye on Miss Evesham, and said in a voice that froze the blood in Miss Evesham's veins:

"Will you come up on to the platform, Miss Evesham?"

Too late did Miss Evesham realise the implication of

William's words: "The human sacrifice must be the person the hypnotised cat belongs to." Before she could collect her senses, a bestial-looking man with gorilla-like arms leapt to her and seized her roughly (for Mr. Westonbury had been tormented all evening by a fear that someone might forestall him in performing the friendly office). Here Miss Evesham's paralysis left her. With a piercing scream she pushed him aside and, turning, fought her way through the crowd to the door. It seemed to her that each member of the audience did his best to bar her progress, but, endowed with superhuman strength (as she said, when describing the affair afterwards), she fought her way to safety. Once outside, she did not stop to look back, but fled as if a hundred devils were at her heels. . . .

Miss Perrott watched the scene with raised eyebrows. A most extraordinary performance, and one best ignored. She had thought for some time that the woman was mental, hanging about her cottage and scowling at her whenever they met.

"Ladies and gentlemen," she began, "the subject on which I am going to speak to you is one which, whether you realise it or not, is of vital importance to you all . . ."

It was William alone who witnessed the next stage in the drama.

Miss Perrott felt a little worried after the meeting. The woman was evidently in the throes of a serious nervous breakdown. It would be only right and neighbourly to call on the way home and ask how she was.

So William, looking out of his bedroom window, saw Miss Perrott in her long black coat, with Hector under her arm, opening the gate of Miss Evesham's garden. The moonlight lent her a sinister air, accentuating her witch-like appearance and giving Hector's eyes a green and wicked light. But even William was not prepared for what happened next. Miss Evesham's window was thrown open and Miss Evesham's voice, raised to a shrill scream, rent the silence of the night: "Get *out*, you she-devil!"

Some heavy object was hurled at Miss Perrott. It missed her but caused her unceremoniously to abandon her neighbourly intentions and make her way homeward as quickly as she could.

Early next morning a taxi drew up at the door of Miss Evesham's house, into which Miss Evesham and her belongings hastily transferred themselves.

Later in the day a furniture van drew up and removed Miss Evesham's furniture.

Later still, William sat down to write to Joan. He had meant to give her a full account of what had happened, but it was a long and complicated story, and William was, at the best, a poor letter-writer.

"DEER JOAN (he wrote),
    "It's orl rite, you can cum bak now.
                                    "luv from
                                        "WILLIAM."

CHAPTER V

THE BATTLE OF FLOWERS

"WE'VE gotter get somethin' ready for Vict'ry," said William. "Everyone else is doin'."

"What sort of thing?" demanded Ginger.

"Some people are gettin' up Vict'ry balls . . ." said Henry.

"We jolly well don't want a Vict'ry ball. Dancin' with rotten ole girls! We get enough of that at the dancin' class. I never have seen what people see in it, dancin'."

"They're gettin' up a pageant where my aunt lives," said Douglas. "She's goin' to be Queen Elizabeth."

"I thouldn't mind bein' her," said Violet Elizabeth graciously. "It wath only 'cauth of mumpth I wathn't her before.

"You won't be in it at all," said William sternly. "No one asked you to the meetin' anyway."

"If Joan can come, why thouldn't I?" demanded Violet Elizabeth.

"'Cause we asked Joan. She helps. You only mess everything up."

Violet Elizabeth looked at Joan who sat, small and shy and earnest, on an upturned packing case in a corner of the old barn.

"Thee's got thoot on her nothe," she remarked dispassionately.

Joan took out her handkerchief and rubbed off the infinitesimal speck.

"We had the chimney sweep this morning," she explained.

"You leave her alone," said William indignantly to Violet Elizabeth.

"I only thaid thee had thoot on her nothe," said Violet Elizabeth with devastating sweetness. "I thought thee'd like to know. I'd like to know if I had thoot on my nothe. Anyway"—she smiled on them serenely—"you can't turn me out. If you try I'll thcream an' thcream an' *thcream*."

William sighed, deciding for the hundredth time that girls complicated every situation into which one admitted them. Joan was a different matter. She lacked the ruthlessness and dominating personality of Violet Elizabeth. She was quiet and amenable and willing to help. She joined the Outlaws as a slave. Violet Elizabeth, despite the disarming camouflage of meekness that she could assume for her own ends, joined it as a tyrant.

"Well, we aren't havin' any girls in whatever we do for this Vict'ry show," said William.

He spoke firmly, but there was something in the curve of Violet Elizabeth's cherubic lips and in the light of her wide blue eyes that made him feel a good deal less confident than he sounded.

"You can help if you want," he added, "but that's jolly well all."

"That'th all we want to do, ithn't it, Joan?" said Violet Elizabeth.

"Yes," agreed Joan earnestly.

"What do they *do* in pageants?" asked William.

"They sort of act things out of hist'ry," said Henry.

"You'll have to have girlth if ith hithtory, William," said Violet Elizabeth with quiet satisfaction. "Hithtory'th full of them—queenth and thingth."

"They sort of act without talkin'," said Henry, ignoring her.

"How do people know what they're actin' if they don't talk?" said William.

"They've jus' gotter guess, I s'pose," said Henry.

"I see," said William thoughtfully. "If a man comes on in a crown, wearin' a rose, it'd be Charles I in the Wars of the Roses, or somethin' like that."

"Yes, somethin' like that," agreed Henry doubtfully, "but I don't think it was Charles I in the Wars of the Roses."

"Well, Charles II, then," said William impatiently. "An' if someone comes on an' puts a coat over a puddle it'd be that man who put his coat down for Queen Elizabeth. The Black Prince, wasn't it?"

"Sir Walter Raleigh," murmured Henry.

"Yes, I knew it was either him or the Black Prince," said William.

"I thaid you'd have to have girlth," said Violet Elizabeth with a radiant smile. "I *thaid* tho."

"Well, we're not goin' to," said William. "I bet I could do Queen Elizabeth all right."

"I'm sure you could," said Joan, but Violet Elizabeth burst into a peal of silvery laughter.

"I'd love to thee you," she said. "You'd look tho funny."

"Anyway, we're not doin' that," said William irritably. "We're not goin' to copy anyone. We're goin' to think out somethin' of our own."

"Sometimes they have someone readin' aloud in po'try what they're actin' while they're actin' it," said Henry, reluctant to leave a subject on which he felt himself to be an authority.

"Well, we're not goin' to have anythin' out of hist'ry," said William firmly. "We get enough of that in school. All that fuss las' week jus' cause I said that ole Caxton invented the steam engine 'stead of Wat Tyler or whoever it was!" Henry opened his mouth to protest then closed it again as William continued: "Anyway, what does it matter what they're called? It's jus' a name their mother happened to think of an' she might jus' as well have thought of somethin' else. I bet she'd have called him Wat Tyler, or whatever it was, if she'd thought of it. I've got an aunt that always calls me Robert an' Robert William an' no one tells her that she's a monument of c'lossal ignorance an' crass stupidity an' all the things ole Markie called me. What does it matter what people's names are, anyway?"

He paused for breath, and Ginger said mildly:

"Well, we aren't any nearer findin' what to do for this Vict'ry show."

"No, but we can jolly well keep off history," said William, in a voice that still held the aftermath of bitterness.

"If it's a Vict'ry show," said Joan, "let's have somethin' about Vict'ry."

"That's a good idea," said William, impressed.

"I wath juth going to thuggetht it," said Violet Elizabeth serenely.

"We could have Britannia," said Joan, "riding in a

sort of chariot. A wheelbarrow would do. Or that box on wheels you've got."

"I'll be Britannia," said Violet Elizabeth. "My mother'th got a Britannia fanthy dreth cothtume."

"You jolly well won't," said William. "If we have girls in it at all, Joan's being Britannia."

"Thee can't be," said Violet Elizabeth. "Thee hathn't got a Britannia fanthy dreth cothtume."

"You could lend her yours, couldn't you?"

"Yeth," said Violet Elizabeth, still smiling serenely. "But I won't. . . ."

"Then you're a rotten mean ole girl."

"And after Britannia we could have some British soldiers," said Joan, hastily intervening before the quarrel could reach such proportions as to hold up progress indefinitely. "We could easily get some boys to be those. And then we could have Germany and captured German prisoners."

"Who'd be them?" said Douglas doubtfully. "I bet no one'd want to be them."

"We could fix that up later," said William. "It's a jolly good idea, anyway." He turned to Violet Elizabeth. "Would you like to be Germany? It's a jolly good part."

"What thould I wear?" said Violet Elizabeth. "It dependth on what I'd wear."

They considered the question.

"Swashtikas," suggested Henry.

"No," said Violet Elizabeth firmly. "I don't like thwathtikath!"

"Sackcloth," said Ginger.

"No," said Violet Elizabeth, still more firmly. "I don't like thackcloth." Suddenly her small face beamed. "*Tell* you what! I've got a fanthy dreth at home I could wear. Ith a fanthy dreth of a rothe. Ith got a thkirt of pink thilk petalth, all thtanding out, and pink thilk thtockingth and thoeth. And ith got a pink rothe-bud for a cap. A couthin of mine had it before the war and thee sent it to me 'cauth thee'd grown out of it and it would juth fit me now. I wouldn't mind being Germany if I could wear that."

"Well, you can't," said William shortly.

"But, William, ith a *pretty* dreth," she assured him earnestly. "You could thow a thwathika on if you like," she conceded. "Thomewhere where it wouldn't thow."

"If you think——" began William portentously, but she interrupted him.

"And I muth ride in the chariot and I muth go on firtht in front of Britannia."

She smiled at them radiantly, as if she had completely solved the problem.

"You can't do that if you're Germany," said William.

"Why not?"

"'Cause—'cause you've gotter be sorry for all the wrong you've done."

"Well, I'm not," said Violet Elizabeth with spirit, "and I haven't done any wrong."

"You started the war."

"I didn't," snapped Violet Elizabeth. "I wath in bed with a billiouth attack the day the war thtarted. Athk the doctor if you don't believe me."

"You're bats," said William. "It's no good talking to you. An' we jolly well don't want you in the show anyway."

"Then you can't have the Britannia cothtume."

"We don't want it," said William untruthfully.

"I don't mind Violet Elizabeth being Britannia," said Joan, anxious that the success of the pageant should not be jeopardised by jealousy among the cast.

"Well, we do," said William. He turned to Violet Elizabeth. "You're not going to be in it, so you can clear off. We've got a lot of things to discuss."

"I'll thtay and lithen to you dithcuthing them," said Violet Elizabeth, with the air of one granting a favour.

"People with manners," said William crushingly, "don't stay where they're not wanted."

"I'm not a perthon with mannerth," said Violet Elizabeth, uncrushed, "and I like thtaying where I'm not wanted. It'th gen'rally more interethting than where I am wanted."

"We'll carry on as if she wasn't there," said William to the others. "She's just not worth taking any notice of. I'm glad she's not going to be in it. She's always more bother than she's worth."

He could not help glancing at Violet Elizabeth as he spoke, hoping to see her look conscience-stricken or at least abashed, but she met his glance with a smile of shattering sweetness.

"Well, now," he went on hastily. "We've got a lot to arrange. Joan'll be Britannia, and we can easily fix up a costume for her with flags and things an' she'll come on in this cart, drawn by two of us, an' we'll write some po'try for someone to say when she comes on. Who can write po'try?" He looked round the circle, carefully avoiding Violet Elizabeth's eye.

"I can thay *Cargoeth*," said Violet Elizabeth proudly.
They ignored her.

"You can, can't you, Joan?" said William.

"I can try," said Joan doubtfully. "I once wrote
a poem about a mouse."

"Thay it," challenged Violet Elizabeth.

Again they ignored her.

"Then we'll get some boys to be soldiers," said
William. "Marchin' an' drillin' and so on. . . ."

"I don't thee what mithe have got to do with a
Victory pageant," said Violet Elizabeth.

"Nobody asked you," said William. "I wish you'd
shut up."

"All right," said Violet Elizabeth, with unexpected
meekness. "I only thought it was thilly thaying
po'try about mithe at a Victory pageant and it *ith*."

"Well, let's get on with things," said William.
There was no doubt that Violet Elizabeth's interrup-
tions had a disintegrating effect on the discussion. It
was difficult to pick up the threads again. "After
these soldiers, we'll have Germany. I bet we'll get
a jolly good Germany an' we'll get a jolly good dress
for whoever it is, too, with sackcloth and swastikas
and things."

"It'th *thuth* a pretty pink thilk dreth, William,"
said Violet Elizabeth wistfully. "It'th got little pearl
beadth thewn on for dew dropth. I don't know why
you won't let me wear it."

"Well, we won't," said William testily. "We only
want you to shut up." He turned to the others.
"Then, after Germany, we'll have the captured German
prisoners . . . I *say*! Couldn't we get Hubert Lane
and his gang to be the captured German prisoners?"

The Outlaws thought of the Hubert Laneites, between whom and the Outlaws a feud had existed as long as any of them could remember.

"They'd make jolly good German prisoners," agreed Ginger, "but I bet they wouldn't do it."

"Couldn't we capture them?"

"If we did, we couldn't keep them till the pageant."

"Let's ask them to do it. Let's make out that it's the most important part. They're jolly stupid."

"Yes, but they're not quite as stupid as that."

"Where shall we have it, anyway? Where do people have pageants?"

"They generally have them in the grounds of castles or big houses," said Henry.

"Our houthe ith the only big houthe in the village," said Violet Elizabeth triumphantly, "an' I won't let you have it in our garden unleth you let me be Britannia and wear my pink thilk dreth, tho there! I don't thuppothe," she added thoughtfully, "that my mother would let you have it there, anyway, 'cauthe thee doethn't like you. Thee thayth that you're rough, an' rude, an' badly behaved, and you *are*, and I'm going home now, and you'll be *thorry* one day that you've been tho nathty to me."

Thereupon, Violet Elizabeth withdrew with an impressive air of dignity which did not quite desert her even when she turned at the door and put out her tongue at them.

"Well, thank goodness she's gone!" said William. "Now we can get on with things a bit."

But their project was still beset with difficulties— Germany, the German prisoners, the scene of the pageant. . . .

"We can't have it at the Hall now Violet Elizabeth's not in it."

"There's the Manor at Marleigh," said Joan.

"They wouldn't let us have it there."

"They're away. I heard my mother saying that Sir Gerald and Lady Markham had shut up the Manor and gone to Scotland. And they've let nearly all the garden to a market gardener at Marleigh. They've only kept the lawn and the part just outside the house and one old gardener."

"That sounds all right," said William, brightening. "An' I bet they won't be there for Vict'ry. They'll go to London for it. High-up people do. I bet he'll be carryin' a banner or holdin' a sceptre or somethin' in the procession. An' I know that ole gardener. He's got an arm-chair in the greenhouse, an' he does his Football Pools there all day, an' he's deaf an' nearly blind, an' never takes any notice of anythin'. He'd probably think we'd got permission. . . ."

This was felt to be a little over-optimistic, but it seemed to be the best plan in the circumstances.

"We'll rehearse ordin'ry in the old barn," said William, "but we'll have the dress rehearsal an' the real show at the Manor. You'll start writin' your po'try, won't you, Joan?" and, with a somewhat confused memory of Violet Elizabeth's strictures, added: "It needn't be about mice, you know."

"Of course not," said Joan, a little irritably. "I only said I once wrote a poem about a mouse."

"An' we'll get some boys for soldiers, an'"—not very hopefully—"I'll try an' fix up with the Hubert Laneites to be German prisoners."

   .   .   .   .   .

He approached Hubert Lane the next day.

"Say, Hubert," he said. "We're goin' to get up a sort of Vict'ry pageant."

Hubert's fat face spread into a grin.

"Yeah?" he said.

There seemed to be something more offensive than usual in the grin, but William ignored it.

"I wonder whether you an' your gang'd like parts in it?"

Again Hubert said: "Yeah?"

"They're the best parts in the show," said William. "We thought it wasn't worth offerin' you anythin' but the best parts. We don't mind takin' the worst parts ourselves 'cause we're gettin' it up an' we don't want the best parts. We want you to have 'em."

"Kind of you," said Hubert, with a sneer, but the sneer was so much his usual expression that, again, William ignored it.

"Well?" he said.

"What parts are they?" said Hubert.

"Jolly important ones," said William. "They're —they're German prisoners."

"Funny, that," said Hubert ruminatively.

"What?"

"I was jus' goin' to ask you an' your gang to be German prisoners in our pageant."

"Your pageant?" said William.

"Yeah," said Hubert, with an intensification of his sneer. "We're gettin' up a Vict'ry pageant. Violet Elizabeth's goin' to be Britannia—her mother's got a jolly good Britannia costume—an' we're goin' to be British soldiers, an' we're goin' to get someone to be Germany, an' we were goin' to ask you to be German prisoners. All you'd need would be a rope tied round your necks. . . ."

William stared at him, speechless with horror. He had not thought even Violet Elizabeth capable of such depths of perfidy. . . .

"It ought to be a jolly good pageant," continued Hubert suavely. "Mrs. Bott's goin' to let us do it on the lawn at the Hall, an' all the children in the village have promised to come. We're goin' to give 'em tea. . . . Well, what about it? Will you be German prisoners? You'd make jolly good German prisoners."

Then, seeing the light of battle in William's eye, he took to flight. William pursued him half-heartedly for a few yards, then returned to break the news to the others.

"She's pinched our pageant an' she's gettin' it up with the Hubert Laneites," he announced. "Would anyone have thought she'd be as mean as that?"

"Yes, I would," said Joan simply.

"What are we goin' to do?" said Ginger.

"We're goin' on with it," said William firmly. "We're not goin' to give it up jus' for a mean ole girl like that. *Gosh!* Would you have thought it? Jus' because she couldn't be Britannia! Sickening! I bet even Hitler wouldn't have done a thing like that."

So, doggedly, they continued their preparations for their pageant, but somehow the zest had gone out of it. It wasn't only the fact of the rival pageant that was being organised and rehearsed in the grounds of the Hall under Violet Elizabeth's despotic rule. It was the absence of Violet Elizabeth herself. They had resented her presence among them and heartily wished her away but, now that she had gone, they missed her—missed her dynamic personality, her unreasonableness, her contrariness, her varying moods, her uncertain temper, even her lisp. . . . Their loyalty to Joan was unchanged, but she was almost too docile and amenable and ready to fall in with their suggestions. She failed to provide the stimulus that Violet Elizabeth had always provided. And, though they would not have admitted it, they felt wounded and betrayed. That Violet Elizabeth, their most troublesome but most loyal follower, should have joined the Hubert Laneites was almost too monstrous for belief.

Joan did her best. She wrote her "poetry" with frowning concentration, sucking her pencil to induce inspiration and drawing it across her forehead in moments of deep thought till her brow resembled a complicated railway map. For the Britannia costume she had decided to stitch flags on to her white frock, but she had not yet been able to obtain any flags. Everyone who had them was keeping them for their own Victory decorations and the village shop was sold out.

"I'm sure to get some before the day," she said. "I expect there'll be heaps in the shop by then."

William concentrated his efforts on drilling his band of soldiers. He had found no difficulty in obtaining recruits. The only difficulty was in organising them. They were apt to scuffle and scrimmage and indulge in horseplay highly unsuitable to British soldiers in a Victory parade. The rehearsals offered an excellent opportunity of paying off private scores and generally ended in a free fight in which everyone joined just for the fun of the thing whether he had any private scores to pay off or not. William tried to divide them into groups of soldiers, sailors, airmen, commandos and paratroops, but the free fight would break out again immediately and the ranks would become inextricably mingled.

"You can't go on like this," he said despairingly, "fightin' all the time."

"That's what soldiers are for, isn't it?" they replied.

"They're for fightin' an enemy, not each other," said William.

"Give us an enemy, then."

"I tried to," said William. "I tried to get the Hubert Laneites, but they wouldn't come."

The Hubert Laneites were keeping well out of the Outlaws' way, while carrying on energetic preparations for their own pageant. The Outlaws watched them from the road through the hedge, as Violet Elizabeth rehearsed them ruthlessly in the garden of the Hall.

"Gosh! She's puttin' 'em through it," said William. "Thank Goodness it's them, not us, now!"

"Thank Goodness!" echoed the Outlaws with relief that did not ring quite true.

Once they met Violet Elizabeth in the road outside the Hall. She passed them without looking at them, head in air. They passed her in silence, refraining by tacit consent from jeers or hostilities. Her treachery went too deep for that. . . .

They gathered that the Hubert Laneites, like themselves, had been unable to persuade anyone to take the parts of Germany or of the German prisoners. Otherwise their preparations were on a lavish scale. Mrs. Bott had promised cakes, lemonade and ice cream. . . .

"I don't see what good it is, goin' on with the thing at all," said Ginger gloomily. "No one'll come to it, anyway, with the Hubert Laneites havin' it at the Hall on the same day an' givin' them tea."

"I'm not goin' to stop it 'cause of *them*," said William firmly. "I'm jolly well goin' on with it, whether anyone comes or not."

The dress rehearsal was fixed for the next Saturday, and the cast assembled in the old barn early in the afternoon. Joan had tried up to the last minute to obtain some flags but without success, and had had to content herself with pinning a red, white and blue rosette and a Royal Engineers' badge on her white frock and putting a green silk tea cosy on her head. She carried a toasting fork for a trident and the costume was considered by the others to be an adequate, if not striking, representation of Britannia. William, as Commander-in-Chief, wore a tin hat and his father's Home Guard boots. The others, who had been told to collect "uniforms" from whatever sources they could, presented a motley spectacle. One wore a fancy dress costume of Robin Hood and carried a poker. Another wore a very ancient fancy dress costume of Henry the Fifth, the coat of mail knitted in dishcloth cotton from which the aluminium paint had long since disappeared, and from which dangled several tempting odds and ends of dishcloth cotton. Another wore a red Indian costume with feathered head-dress. Another, who had once taken part in a charade as an Ancient Briton, wore a fur rug, with a tray for a shield. One wore a gas mask, another a saucepan, another a fire guard. . . .

Putting an end, as well as he could, to the inevitable skirmish, William addressed them in his most impressive manner.

"Now look here," he said. "Stop messin' about an' listen to me. We're goin' over to Marleigh Manor for the dress rehearsal an'—stop bangin' your tray, Victor Jameson—an' we'll go by the fields an' keep by the hedge 'cause we don't want a lot of people seein' us—stop blowin' that trumpet, George Bell—an' we'll go on to the lawn through the shrub'ry from the road an' do it under the tree at the end of the lawn same as we said—stop pullin' the fur out of his rug, Ginger. He told you it'd got the moth in—an' I bet it'll be all right with it bein' Sat'day. That ole gardener always takes Sat'day off, so we can go right through the pageant without bein' int'rupted. Stop unwinding his coat of mail, Freddie Parker. I don't care if you are windin' it into a nice ball. What's he goin' to do with only about an inch of coat of mail left? Now get into line—Joan first, then me, then the rest of you—an' don't make so much noise. We don't want everyone knowin' about it before the day."

It had been decided to dispense with the chariot for the dress rehearsal, so Joan, looking solemn and intense in her white dress and green tea cosy, the exercise book containing her "poetry" under her arm, set off at the head of the procession. William followed, leading his motley band of warriors, still scuffling and scrimmaging but in a more subdued manner.

They climbed the hill to Marleigh by way of the fields, keeping to the shadow of the hedge, as William had directed, and attracting no attention except from an old horse, who gazed at them with an expression of

"I'VE GOT A LOVELY THURPRITHE FOR YOU, WILLIAM,"
SAID VIOLET ELIZABETH.

incredulous amazement and then uttered a neigh that
sounded like a burst of derisive laughter.

"Shut up!" said William. "You look a jolly sight
funnier than we do, anyway."

They made their way through the shrubbery and
on to the front lawn of Marleigh Manor.

And there they had their first shock.

For the lawn was full of children—bored, listless-
looking children—sitting in serried rows facing the
empty space under the copper beech where William
had planned to hold his pageant. For a few moments
he was much too taken aback to do anything but stare
at them; then, reacting automatically to the situation,
he led his band on to the open space and started
proceedings.

"Ladies an' gentlemen," he began. "This is our
Vict'ry pageant, an' this is Joan—I mean Britannia.
Go on, Joan."

Joan opened her book, glanced at it for a moment
or two to refresh her memory, and began her recital.

"I am Britannia, ruling the waves
And Britons that never, never, never,
Never shall be slaves."

She stood aside and motioned forward the motley
band of warriors.

"These are British soldiers that won the war
And aren't going to fight any more.
Soldiers on land and sailors on the seas
And commandos jumping down from trees,
And paratroops coming down from the skies,
And now the war's over it's going to be very nice."

Here each branch of the services, as drilled by William, was to have given a display of its particular activity. The soldiers were to march and make a show of shooting with imaginary rifles, the sailors to scan the horizon with imaginary telescopes, commandos and paratroops to swarm up the copper beech and drop lightly from its branches. This had never yet gone according to plan, and it was obvious that it was not going to do so to-day. In fact, the usual scrimmage was just in process of forming itself, when——

The Outlaws received their second shock.

For Violet Elizabeth, dressed in her pink silk rose costume, appeared at the head of the Hubert Laneites and led them up to William, smiling radiantly.

"I wath only teathing you, William," she said. "I've got a lovely thurprithe for you."

She turned the radiant smile on to the audience and, striking an attitude, proclaimed:

"An' I am Germany, an' thethe"—pointing to the Hubert Laneites—"are German prithonerths. I've not made a piethe of poetry about mithe, but I could if I tried."

The Hubert Laneites glared at her in impotent fury, aghast at the trick she had played on them.

For Violet Elizabeth had joined them, offering to organise their pageant and play the part of Britannia, and even help them capture the Outlaws for German prisoners. She had insisted on wearing the rose costume instead of the Britannia one because she said that pink suited her better than red, white and blue. Finally she had told them that the Outlaws were having their dress rehearsal to-day, and had per-suaded them that it would be an easy matter to break it up and force the Outlaws to play the part of German prisoners. Instead of which she had shamelessly delivered them into the hands of their enemies, making them play the hateful and humiliating part themselves in the Outlaws' pageant.

She stood there, smiling proudly.

"Ithn't it a lovely thurprithe, William?" she said.

The infuriated Hubert Laneites flung themselves upon the Outlaws. The Outlaws flung themselves upon the Hubert Laneites. The battle spread to the audience, and the audience, losing its air of listlessness, flung itself upon both sides impartially.

Struggling masses of children surged to and fro over the lawn. Hubert Lane dodged round the summer house with William in hot pursuit. A member of the audience had got Bertie Franks down on the ground and was filling his mouth with grass. Claude Bellew (another Hubert Laneite) was half-way up the copper beech with Ginger hanging on to his leg and trying to pull him down. Henry the Fifth was wrestling with his own disintegrating costume, his ankles pinioned by yards of tangled dishcloth cotton. The peaceful summer air was rent by shouts and yells and war-whoops.

Then a sudden silence fell.

Lady Markham was making her way to them over the lawn from the house.

And here the Outlaws got their third shock.

For she was smiling in unmistakable welcome. She held out her hand to William and clasped his warmly.

"Thank you, my dear boy," she said. "*Thank* you."

Every summer Sir Gerald and Lady Markham invited a party of slum children to spend an afternoon in the grounds and partake of a tea that had continued even in wartime to be comparatively lavish. They were a conscientious couple, deeply sensible of their obligations to the community in general and, though they had closed the Manor and were spending the summer in Scotland, they decided to come back for the usual Saturday of the children's visit and do the thing in style, as they had always done. They had prepared the lavish tea. They had engaged a conjuror to do conjuring tricks on the lawn. They had engaged a Punch and Judy show to follow. And then, when the audience had arrived—shy and ill-at-ease and even slightly resentful, as it generally was at first—the conjuror rang up to say that he had sprained his ankle, and a few minutes later the Punch and Judy man rang up to say that he was down with 'flu. Lady Markham telephoned every entertainment agency she knew. No one was free on such short notice. Frantically she rang up all her friends. None of them had any suggestions except one who offered to recite passages from Shakespeare, and another who offered to give a lecture on "Home Life in the Eighteenth Century" which she had given at the Women's Institute the week before and which had, she said, been well received by the few who had turned up to listen to it. Meantime the audience sat, bored and impassive, waiting. . . .

And then the miracle had happened.

"I don't know who sent the children," said Lady Markham afterwards. "Or whether it was their own idea. They must, of course, have heard of the dilemma I was in, because I'd simply rung up everyone I knew to tell them about it. I was feeling simply *desperate*, when I looked out of the window and saw these children coming to my rescue. It really was a charming idea. A children's Battle of Flowers. First came a little girl dressed as a snowdrop, followed by her pages, then came a little girl dressed as a rose, followed by her pages. The pages, of course, were rather strangely dressed, but, considering the war and everything, it was excellent. Then they started this Battle of the Flowers and invited the audience to join in, and then the whole thing went like a house on fire. It became just a little bit rough, I admit, but the children enjoyed it and that was the chief thing."

"Splendid effort, my boy," said Sir Gerald, grasping William's hand in his turn. "Simply splendid! I can't tell you how grateful my wife and I are to you. . . . Ice broken all right now, eh?"

The ice was certainly broken, together with most of the chairs and benches on which the audience had been sitting, but host and hostess gazed at the chaos with smiles of unalloyed pleasure.

"Such a relief!" said Lady Markham. "These afternoons have always been a success. I should have been miserable if this one had been a failure. You and your friends will stay to tea, won't you, and help us till the little visitors go?"

Dazedly William promised that he would. Dazedly he returned to the fray. The Battle of Flowers had developed into a game which everyone played according to his own rules, and in which everyone seemed to know what he was doing, though no one else did. The little visitors leapt and screamed and shouted and pushed.

"It's the best party we've ever 'ad here," said one of them to William. "I'm jolly glad they asked you."

They clustered round the trestle tables in the hall, dishevelled and panting, and began the attack upon jellies, sandwiches, cakes, buns. Sir Gerald and Lady Markham hovered gratefully about William, pressing delicacies upon him.

"It really is good of you, you know " said Sir Gerald, "giving up your Saturday afternoon to getting us out of a hole like this."

William grinned sheepishly and took another slab of chocolate cake.

Violet Elizabeth and Joan stood on one side and watched proceedings with an air of aloofness, daintily nibbling chocolate biscuits.

"It's a very pretty frock," said Joan generously.

"Yourth ith pretty, too," said Violet Elizabeth, not to be outdone in generosity, and added. "An' yourth wath a very nithe piethe of poetry."

"I 'spect you could have done one just as good," said Joan.

"Yeth, I 'thpect I could," said Violet Elizabeth complacently.

They watched the boys scuffling round the table, wolfing the lavish tea.

"Jutht look at them," said Violet Elizabeth, elevating her small nose. "Aren't they dithguthting?"

"They haven't any manners, boys," said Joan.

The two felt themselves to be withdrawn into a rarified atmosphere of feminine superiority.

"They haven't any mannerth and they haven't any thenth," said Violet Elizabeth severely. "I

F

thay, will you come to tea at our houthe to-morrow, and we won't have any boyth?"

"Yes, I'd like to," said Joan.

William approached them, his mouth still full of chocolate cake.

"We're goin' out to play rounders," he said indistinctly. "Come on."

Violet Elizabeth looked at him disdainfully.

"What a meth you're in!" she said, with an odious imitation of grown-up disapproval. "Joan and I don't care for thothe childith gameth. We're going to walk round the garden, aren't we, Joan?"

"Yes," said Joan.

They walked off, arm in arm, without looking back.

William stood staring after them, baffled and crestfallen, pondering on the incomprehensibility of the female sex. Then he shrugged his shoulders, dismissed the problem, and ran to join the riot on the lawn. . . .

CHAPTER VI

ESMERALDA TAKES A HAND

WILLIAM was finding life rather interesting. His home was in the hands of "the decorators," and William was enjoying the experience. It didn't matter how untidy you were because everything was all over the place anyway, and you never knew where you were going to sleep. He had even offered to sleep in the coal cellar, so that he could pretend to be a stowaway on a ship, but the offer had been refused. He had slept, last night, on a camp-bed in the dining-room with his air-gun by his side, because he understood that thieves always gained access to a house by the dining-room window, but his rest had been broken by nothing more exciting than a miauling cat. Still, in spite of these disappointments, he enjoyed the importance that the position gave him among his friends and did his best to convey the impression that the workmen accepted his help and deferred to his judgment with gratitude and humility.

He was holding forth now to the three other Outlaws in the garden of his house, while Jumble, his mongrel dog, occupied himself by burying a paint brush that he had found among the workmen's things in the garage. It was an odd sort of bone, thought Jumble, and had a peculiar taste, but he hoped it would improve with keeping. . . .

"I told 'em I thought it would be a jolly good idea to put distemper on the furniture, too," said William. "It'd make it look a bit more exciting. Wood's jus' brown an' brown's a jolly dull colour."

"Did they do it?" said Ginger with interest.

"Well," said William evasively, "they said they'd think about it. I bet they'll do it in the end. Come on in an' have a look. All the wrong furniture's in the wrong rooms. It's wizard. It's like bein' on a desert island an' havin' things washed up."

They entered the house. It was empty. The workmen had been called away to another job, and Mrs. Brown had not yet returned from her morning's shopping.

"Look!" said William proudly. "There's no stair-carpet, an' I bet none of you can make as much noise as what I can, goin' upstairs. Come on. Let's try it."

They tried it. . . . The echoes had not yet died away when they entered Mr. Brown's dressing-room. Jumble, excited by the crescendo of their ascent and considering himself a not unworthy contributor to it, set to work on one of Mr. Brown's bedroom slippers. He'd had an idea for some time that the lining would come right out if he took enough trouble over it.

"They're not started here yet," said William, looking round the room, "but I 'spect they're goin' to. Look! There's the distemper stuff."

They gazed down at the pail of distemper that stood in front of the chest-of-drawers.

"I bet they're goin' to distemper that chest-of-drawers," went on William. "I could see they thought it was a jolly good idea when I s'gested it. I don't

know why no one's ever thought of it before. I bet
I've invented somethin' that'll make me famous in
hist'ry."

"I think it'd look a bit funny with distemper on,"
said Henry judicially.

"It wouldn't," retorted William.

"I bet distemper wouldn't stay on," said Ginger.
"It'd slip off."

"It wouldn't."

"It would."

"It wouldn't."

"It would."

"All right. I'll show you."

"You'd better not, William," said Douglas nervously.

But William had, for the moment, lost touch with
reality. He was an inventor determined to justify his
faith, an artist inspired by an ideal.

"Look!" he said, and, before even he himself quite
realised what he was doing, he had taken the brush
that lay beside the pail, plunged it into the pail and
drawn a long sweeping line over the chest-of-drawers.

"Gosh!" said the Outlaws.

"Well, of course, it looks a bit queer like that,"
admitted William. "It'll look all right when the brown
doesn't show."

He dipped the brush into the distemper again and
drew it once more over the wood. But something of
his enthusiasm was fading, and a look of anxiety had
come into his face.

"Oh, well," he said, glancing round uneasily,
"p'raps we'd better be goin' now. I mean, it looks
jolly fine, but p'raps—anyway, p'raps we'd better be
goin'. Come on, Jumble."

He retrieved the slipper, replaced the lining as best he could, put it with its fellow and turned to the door. Their descent of the uncarpeted stairs was more hasty and less re-echoing than their ascent had been. There was even a suggestion of flight in its precipitancy. . . .

Something of William's uneasiness left him as he reached the open air.

"It's a jolly good idea," he said, "but I 'spect I'll have to get people used to it gradual."

Jumble, now freely bespattered with distemper as a result of William's recent operations, was investigating every plant with patient thoroughness, trying to remember where he'd buried his paint brush.

"What's that?" said Ginger suddenly, looking at a shrouded shape inside the greenhouse.

"Oh, that's Ethel's dummy thing," explained William. "She calls it Esmeralda. Dunno why. It's like a person, but it hasn't got a head, an' she uses it when she's makin' dresses."

"But why's it in the greenhouse?" said Henry.

"Oh, well," said William, "they kept movin' it about from one room to another an' bits of plaster an' stuff kept fallin' on it an' she was afraid of the dress she was makin' gettin' spoiled, so she said she'd keep it down here in the greenhouse till the men had gone."

"Why's it got a sheet over it?" said Douglas. "Makes it look like a ghost."

"It's to keep that ole dress she's makin' clean," said William. "It looks jus' like a person when it's got a dress on it, 'cept for its head. Come on in an' have a look at it. The door's locked, but I know where they keep the key."

He took the key from the ledge above the door and

unlocked it. They trooped into the greenhouse and stood gazing at the shrouded form of Esmeralda.

"Ethel'll be mad if she finds us here," said Douglas.

"Well, she won't find us," said William, "'cause she's gone to stay with Peggy Barton while her room's bein' papered. Look!" He removed the sheet and revealed a willowy shape encased in grey *crêpe de Chine*. "That's how she does it. She jus' makes them on it same as if it was a real person 'cept it can't feel pins. She's been in a jolly bad temper over this one."

"Why?" said Henry.

"'Cause she had a row with Jimmy Moore over it, an' it always makes her in a bad temper when she has a row with Jimmy Moore."

"What did she have a row with him about?"

"He wanted her to go to the pictures with him, an' she said she wouldn't 'cause she wanted to finish the dress, an' they both got mad at each other."

"Why?" said Douglas.

"'Cause they're both bats," said William, summing up the situation as simply and concisely as he could.

Then he drew the sheet over the dummy and threw a slightly uneasy glance towards the house.

"P'raps we'd better not mess about with things any more," he said. "Let's go to the old barn an' have a meeting."

"What about?" said Henry.

"Well, there's a lot of things we could have a meeting about," said William. "There's Hubert Lane. I bet he's not stopped laughing at us yet. We've got to do something about Hubert Lane."

In the intermittent warfare that had been waged between the Outlaws and Hubert Lane ever since any of them could remember, Hubert did not often score, but he had scored last week. He had "borrowed" a bear skin rug, with head attached, that belonged to his mother and hidden it—and himself—in a bush when the Outlaws were coming through the wood at dusk. The ferocious-looking head, with bared teeth, just protruded from the leafage, and the growl that Hubert uttered was so blood-curdling that the Outlaws had taken to their heels without further investigation and fled for the safety of the road.

"What can we do?" asked Henry.

"That's what we've got to plan," said William. "We've got to fix up some sort of trick to pay him back an'——"

"Gosh! Here he is!" said Ginger.

Hubert had just turned the bend in the road and was coming towards them. There was a triumphant smirk on his flabby face.

"Hello," he said, stopping irresolutely, his short fat body poised for flight, should his foes show signs of immediate hostility. But William had decided on subtler methods.

"Hello," he said.

"Where are you going?" said Hubert.

"Mind your own business. Where are you going?"

"Mind your own business."

This conventional opening did not imply any particular rancour, and the conversation would seem to have reached an *impasse*, but Hubert was the sort of boy who must boast about something even if he hadn't anything much to boast about. He dared not, at such close quarters, refer to his bear skin trick, but he had a piece of news to impart that he imagined would increase his prestige, and Hubert thought a lot about his prestige.

"My mother and me's going out to tea to the Grange to Mrs. Warwick's," he said. "She's got her sister staying with her and her sister's a high-up person. She writes stories."

"Yes, I know," said William. "Ethel's met her, an' anyway, it's nothin' to write stories. I write stories myself an' I bet mine are a jolly sight better than hers."

"I bet they're not."

"I bet they are," said William. "I bet she's never had four murders an' three burglaries an' a train accident an' an aeroplane crash an' a man havin' his head pulled off by a gorilla all in one story, has she?"

"I dunno," said Hubert, somewhat deflated by this wealth of invention. "Anyway, I'm going to have a jolly good tea there. The only thing is——" The smirk faded from his face, and a look of apprehension came into it. It was clear that Hubert was worried about something and wanted to confide in them. There was a vein of simplicity beneath Hubert's cunning that the Outlaws had often found useful.

"What?" said William encouragingly.

"Well," said Hubert, "our gardener says it's haunted by the ghost of a woman what once lived there and pined away 'cause the man she was fond of went to Jamaica or somewhere and never came back."

"Well, I wouldn't come back if I went to Jamaica," said Ginger. "There's bananas there."

"An' that's silly," said Henry; "there aren't any ghosts."

"Yes, there are," said Hubert earnestly. "I've met people that've met people that've actu'ly *seen* them.

They look jus' like real people but sort of—sort of "— he shuddered—"*shadowy*."

"Well, anyway, only very old houses are haunted," said Henry, "and The Grange isn't a very old house."

"No, but it's built where an old house used to be," said Hubert, "an' when Mrs. Warwick's father was having that conservatory place built on it they found lots of bits of the old house."

"Well, you won't be havin' tea in the conserv'try."

"No, but the drawing-room's next door to it. There's only a sort of glass door between. I've a good mind not to go. I could pretend to have' flu. I'm jolly good at pretendin' I've got 'flu."

"I keep tellin' you," said Henry, "there aren't any such things as ghosts."

"An' you're a silly baby to be frightened of them if there are," said Ginger.

The smirk returned to Hubert's fat pale face.

"Oh yeah?" he said. He climbed the stile that separated the road from the field and, with the barrier of the stile between him and his foes, gave a jeering laugh. "Yah! You wouldn't be afraid of ghosts, would you? You weren't afraid of an ole fur rug, were you? Yah!"

With that he turned and ran as fast as his fat legs could carry him across the field and towards his home.

The Outlaws stood gazing after him.

"We could catch him easy," said Ginger wistfully.

"No, we won't try," said William. "It wouldn't be any fun anyway. What we've got to do is to fix up a trick for him—an' a better trick than the one he played on us." He stood for a moment deep in thought, then the complicated maze of wrinkles cleared from his brow and a slow smile spread over his face. "*Tell* you what!"

They gathered round him eagerly.

"Yes?"

"I've got an idea an' it's a jolly good one. Listen. He said he was frightened of ghosts an' you know you said that thing of Ethel's in the greenhouse was jus' like a ghost. Well, if we could fix it up. . . ."

"Gosh! We *couldn't* do that," said Douglas in horror.

"Yes, we could," said William, his purpose hardening, as it always did, in the face of opposition. "We could fix it up in the conserv't'ry place he was talkin' about. I've seen it an' it's got a lot of big plants in it. Palm trees an' things. Well, we could put this ghost in with them an' it'd make it look sort of shadowy, same as he said they looked. He'd be scared out of his life. He'd think it was that woman that died of eatin' pineapples."

"She didn't die of eatin' pineapples," said Henry. "She pined away."

"Well, it comes to the same thing," said William impatiently. "Anyway, you can't say it isn't a jolly good idea."

"It's goin' to be a bit diff'cult," said Ginger slowly.

"I bet it ends by gettin' us into a muddle," said Douglas.

"That's right," said William in exasperation. "Start makin' objections the minute I get a good idea, same as you always do. All right, think of a better one if you don't like this." He paused for a second, then continued with an air of triumph: "There! You can't. I knew you couldn't. All right, if you don't want to do it, I'll do it myself."

"Oh, no," said Ginger hastily. "I only said it was goin' to be diff'cult."

"We don't axshully want *not* to do it," said Henry.

"After all," said Douglas philosophically, "we gen'rally get in muddles whatever we do, so it won't make much diff'rence."

They retraced their steps to the greenhouse. William threw a cautious glance at the house as he opened the back gate, but no one seemed to be about. They entered the greenhouse, removed the sheet from Esmeralda and examined her critically.

"The dress is all right," said William. "It's sort of grey and shadowy like a ghost, but it ought to have a head."

"I've heard of ghosts without heads," said Henry. "They carry them under their arm."

"Well, it hasn't got an arm," said Ginger. "At least," holding up the empty grey sleeve that hung from Esmeralda's shapely shoulder, "it's not strong enough to carry a head."

"'Sides," said William, "if we're going to have a head at all we might as well fix it on its neck same as anyone else's."

"Yes," said Ginger, "you remember Hubert said they looked like real people but sort of shadowy, so it's got to have a head if it's goin' to look like a real person."

"*Tell* you what!" said William.

"Yes?"

"I've got that old football upstairs. It's about the size of a head. We could fix it on. . . ."

"Ethel will be mad," Douglas warned him.

"No, we'll be jolly careful," said William. "We won't do it any harm."

"How'll we fix it on?" said Henry.

It was obvious that, as usual, they had become infected by William's optimism and that, despite secret misgivings, they were now definitely committed to the scheme.

"I know!" said William excitedly. "There's some cement upstairs that the workmen were using 'cause some of the tiles in the fireplace were loose. I'll go an' get some. You'd better stay here. It may be jus' a bit dangerous if anyone's found that chest-of-drawers."

But no one had found it. The workmen were still absent, and his mother had not yet returned from her shopping. In a few minutes he rejoined them, carrying a football and a handful of wet cement. Jumble, who had accompanied him, was prancing at his heels, his patches of distemper now hidden by a fine dusting of cement.

"Here it is!" said William. "I'm 'fraid I made a bit of a mess upstairs, I knocked over the bag of cement and some of the water got spilt, but I'll clear it up when we come back."

They watched with interest as he rammed the handful of cement on Esmeralda's neck, then fixed the football on to it.

"There, that's all right," he said, holding the football in position. "I told you it would be."

"It doesn't look much like a person," said Ginger, doubtfully.

"N-no," admitted William, "p'raps it doesn't, but," seeing his handiwork through the indulgent eyes of its creator, "it's more or *less* like a person. I mean, you'd sort of know it was *meant* to be a person, an' I bet a hat'll make all the diff'rence."

"A hat!" said Douglas, aghast. "Gosh! You're not goin' to take one of her hats, are you?"

"I won't do it any harm," William assured him. "I'll take great care of it."

"It'll look a bit queer even in a hat," said Henry.

"No, it won't," said William. "This hat I'm thinkin' of's got a sort of veil that comes all over it an' hangs down."

"Yes, but people'll be able to see there isn't a face through it," said Ginger.

"Y-yes," admitted William, obviously reluctant to see any flaws in his masterpiece, "but it's a *sort* of face. It's brown, but it might be a sort of *sunburnt* face. I've seen people with brown faces when they'd been on holidays."

"Yes, but they've got mouths an' noses an' things. You can't have even sunburnt faces without mouths an' noses an' things."

William frowned, torn between irritation at their criticisms and a secret suspicion that they were justified. Then his brow cleared.

"*Tell* you what!" he said. "There's that mask we had for Guy Fawkes day. That's a *face* all right."

"It's a jolly funny sort of face," said Ginger. "It's got a moustache on it."

"Well, we could take the moustache off," said William. "I bet if we took the moustache off it'd look jus' like that woman that died of pineapples."

"I can see that muddle comin' nearer an' nearer," said Douglas.

"That's right, start grumblin' again," said William bitterly. "Look. If a body with clothes an' a head an' a face an' a hat doesn't make a *person*, I don't

know what does.   An' if you don't want to get even
with Hubert Lane over that bear trick——"

"Yes, we do," they clamoured.   "'Course we do."

"All right," said William, appeased by their eager-
ness.   "Well, it'll be nearly dark at tea-time, so it
won't look as queer as what it looks now.   Pers'nally,
I think it looks all right now, but when it's got its face
an' its hat I bet no one'd know it from a real person."

"When shall we start?" said Henry.

"Well, Hubert said they were goin' to tea, so I
'spect they'll be there about four—that's the time that
grown-ups go out to tea—so we'll get ole Esmeralda
fixed up in the conserv't'ry by four o'clock.   We'll
fix it up so's it'll jus' show through the palm trees an'
things an' so's Hubert will see it.   He'll see it all right,
'cause he'll be lookin' out for a ghost an' the others
won't 'cause they won't be."

So confident did William sound that all of them,
except Douglas, felt their doubts beginning to vanish.

"Yes," said Ginger, "that ought to be all right."

"'Course it will be," said William.   "Well, we'll
meet here at half-past three an' take it along."

"Yes, if somethin' doesn't go wrong before then,"
said Douglas.

But nothing did go wrong before then.   The workmen had not returned from the other job and the
embellishment of Mr. Brown's chest-of-drawers had not
been discovered.   By quarter to four Esmeralda was
complete with mask (from which the moustache had
been removed) hat and veil, and Jumble (whom
experience had proved to be an unsatisfactory con-
spirator) safely shut up indoors.   Even William,
optimist though he was, had had to admit that the

concrete base on which Esmeralda's head rested failed
to conform with the conventional idea of a human
neck, but he had solved the problem by a fur necklet
"borrowed" from his mother.

The Outlaws considered the final result in silence.

"Yes, it doesn't look too bad," said Ginger at
last, a little uncertainly.

"It'll prob'ly look better when we've got a bit more
used to it," said Henry.

"I don't see how we're goin' to get it there," said
Douglas.

"No, you wouldn't," said William crushingly.
"You're jus' a reg'lar Job's blanket. Well, it's quite
easy. We're goin' to take it in my truck."

William's "truck" was an ancient wooden box on
wheels that figured regularly in their games as chariot,
caravan, waggon, battleship, aeroplane, tank and
Rolls Royce. It was fetched from the garage and
Esmeralda, wrapped in her sheet, laid in it carefully.
The whole of the upper part of her body protruded
from the truck, but, steadied by Ginger, Henry and
Douglas, and pushed slowly and carefully by William,
it remained more or less in position. And so, pursued
by shrill barks of protest from the captive Jumble,
the strange procession began to wend its way to The
Grange.

Nothing untoward happened to mar the smooth
running of their plan. Dusk was falling. The road
was empty. . . . Only a passing motorist stared at
them in amazement, turning round to watch them with
such interest that he nearly ran into a telegraph pole.

The gate of The Grange was open, the drive was
empty, the glass door of the conservatory conveniently

WILLIAM CARRIED THE LONG-SUFFERING ESMERALDA
INTO THE DRAWING-ROOM.

ajar. They felt almost awed by the ease with which the whole thing had so far been accomplished.

"Told you it'd be all right," said William jauntily.

"It's not over yet," said Douglas.

"Oh, shut up," said William. "Now let's leave the truck an' the sheet in these bushes an' take Esmeralda into the conserv't'ry. Look! We'll fix her up behind this palm tree, then Hubert'll see it all right, but not too plain. She's a jolly good ghost."

They steered Esmeralda through a forest of tall plants and ornamental stone animals and set her up behind a particularly luxuriant palm.

It was just as they were setting her up that the first mishap occurred.

"Gosh!" said Douglas. "Look!"

They looked. . . . A man had emerged from the greenhouse and was making his way across the lawn in a line that led straight to the conservatory door.

"Crumbs!" said William. "He's comin' here. Quick! You all hide behind the plants an' things an' I—I——" His eye darted round. An open glass door led from the conservatory to the drawing-room. It seemed the only way of escape. "I'll take Esmeralda in there jus' till he's gone an' then I'll bring her back here an' we'll fix her up again."

As quickly as he could he half-carried, half-led the long suffering Esmeralda through the glass door into the drawing-room, setting her up in a corner of the room near the fireplace, hastily straightening hat, veil and fur, so that, if the gardener did chance to catch a glimpse of her, he would think she was a visitor.

And then—almost before he knew what was happening—the other door opened and a woman appeared.

She was a woman whom William had never seen before, but he realised that she was Miss Slater, the sister who was staying with Mrs. Warwick and whom Mrs. Lane and Hubert had been asked to meet. She gave a start of surprise as her eye fell upon William and his charge.

"Oh . . . It's Mrs. Lane and Hubert, isn't it?" she said. "I'm Miss Slater, Mrs. Warwick's sister. I'm so glad that you were able to come and I do hope you haven't been waiting long. The maid never told me you were here."

At that point, much to William's relief, a telephone-bell cut sharply through the air.

"Excuse me one minute," said Miss Slater. "Do sit down. I won't be long, but I must just . . ."

She vanished, closing the door behind her. Once more William's eye darted round. The gardener was pottering about the conservatory. There were no signs of the other Outlaws, but they were probably concealed behind the banks of ferns that ran round the sides of the room. Miss Slater's voice could be heard telephoning in the hall. Every retreat was cut off.

Near the fireplace was a sofa and over the back of the sofa a rug. William's mind worked quickly. He laid Esmeralda down on the sofa and covered her with the rug so completely that only the hat was visible. It was a smart hat, crowned by an ornament that resembled a slightly dissolute dragon-fly. No sooner had he finished arranging the rug than the door opened and Miss Slater reappeared. She gazed in amazement at the prostrate Esmeralda.

"Oh, Mrs. Lane!" she said, then, as there was no

response from the figure on the sofa, turned to William. "Whatever's happened to your mother, Hubert?"

William bared his teeth in a glassy smile.

"Oh, she's all right, but she's jus' not feelin' very well. I mean, she's jus' got to lie down for a few minutes an' not talk."

"Oh, dear!" said Miss Slater, gazing in consternation at the dragon-fly. "I do hope she hasn't got 'flu. Perhaps I'd better send for the doctor."

"Oh, no," said William hastily, "she doesn't want the doctor. She's not got 'flu. She's all right lyin' down an' not talkin'. It's just somethin' that she—she gets."

"A migraine, perhaps?"

"Yes, that," said William gratefully.

"There's a lot of 'flu about. My sister's in bed with it, and of course your mother rang up this morning to say that she was afraid you were starting it and might not be able to come. She was quite well this morning herself?"

"Oh, yes," said William, "she was all right this morning. It comes on quite sudden, this—this thing you said, an', if she lies down under a rug an' doesn't speak, it goes quite sudden. She's better if she's left alone in a room. 'Cept for me, I mean. What I mean is"—he was evidently anxious to make his point quite clear—"if other people are there it takes longer to go."

"I see," said Miss Slater, edging her way to the door with an air of apprehension. "Well, we were going to have tea in the morning room, anyway, so I'll just leave your mother in peace for a few minutes. Won't you come and have some tea, dear?"

"No, thanks," said William, repeating the glassy smile. "I'd better stay with her. She—she comes round easier if I'm here."

Miss Slater withdrew, closed the door and went to the morning-room. Tea was laid on a low table by the fire, and, sitting down, she poured out a cup. She felt in need of stimulant. Almost immediately the door opened and Ethel entered.

"The front door was open so I came in," she said.

"Oh, my dear," said Miss Slater, "I'm so glad to see you. I'm having a most harassing day. My sister's in bed with 'flu and Mrs. Lane and Hubert are in the drawing-room and Mrs. Lane's just had one of those turns she evidently has."

"I didn't know she had turns," said Ethel.

"Well, migraines or seizures or whatever they are," said Miss Slater. "She's lying down on the sofa. Hubert said she'd be all right if she lay down a bit. I'll take her a cup of tea in a minute and see how she is. It's all very distracting. Do sit down and have a cup of tea yourself, my dear. How's the family?"

"I don't know," said Ethel, sitting down and taking her cup of tea. "I'm staying with the Bartons, you know, while my room's being done up. I'm just going along to visit the old home now and see how it's getting on, and the Bartons are giving a little cocktail party next Saturday and they want to know if you and your sister can come along, so I said I'd call on my way home and ask you."

"Oh, thank you, dear," said Miss Slater, "I'd love to but I don't know about my sister. She's got quite a bad attack of 'flu."

"I'm so sorry. No wonder you're feeling harassed."

"That's the least of it, my dear. You see, she'd asked Mrs. Lane and Hubert to tea to-day and this morning Mrs. Lane rang up to say that she thought Hubert was starting 'flu and they mightn't be able to come, so I told her to leave it and just come if she could. Well, she came and had this turn in the drawing-room. My dear, what an odd-looking woman she is!"

"Yes, I suppose so," said Ethel vaguely. "I've known her for so long that I never think about it, but I suppose she *is* odd-looking."

"The room was rather dark, of course," said Miss Slater, "and I'm a little short-sighted, but she seemed to me the most peculiar-looking woman I've ever seen in my life. . . . Hubert appears to be the most devoted little son."

"I shouldn't have thought so," said Ethel.

"Oh, yes, he wouldn't leave her for a minute even to come and have his tea. . . . It's just occurred to me, dear. Does she drink?"

"I've never heard that she does."

"Oh, well, I suppose I'd better go and see how she is and take her a cup of tea."

"I'll take it to her," said Ethel.

"Thank you, dear. I feel a little upset by the whole thing."

Ethel took the cup of tea and went to the drawing-room. Esmeralda still lay on the sofa, but there was no sign of William. William, hearing Ethel's voice, had plunged behind the sofa, where he was crouching, his face already practising its expression of injured— and slightly imbecile—innocence, the words "Well, I didn't *mean* any harm," already forming on his lips.

But Ethel had evidently little interest in Hubert. She drew a small table to the side of the sofa, then looked down at its shrouded occupant.

"How are you, Mrs. Lane?" she said.

Esmeralda made no answer.

"Here's a cup of tea," said Ethel. "I'm so sorry you're ill."

But there was a far-away note in her voice. Her eyes were fixed on the dragon-fly which was almost all that could be seen of the shrouded figure. Almost, but not quite. From beneath the rug a fold of grey *crêpe de Chine* protruded. Ethel's face stiffened. A glazed look came into her eyes. Like one walking in her sleep, she made her way back to the morning-room.

"How is she, dear?" said Miss Slater.

"I don't know," said Ethel. "She didn't say. I think she's gone to sleep."

"That ought to do her good," said Miss Slater. "I suppose I must go in and see her again soon."

"I'll go for you," said Ethel.

She must make sure that the sight she had just seen was reality and no nightmare. The hat, of course, had been advertised in a London paper and she'd sent for it by post. The grey material had been displayed in the window of Mallet's in Hadley marked fifteen and six a yard. Mrs. Lane must have seen the same advertisement and sent for the same hat. She must have seen the material in Mallet's and bought a dress length, as Ethel herself had done. It was difficult to believe that such things could happen in a world governed by a merciful Providence . . . but it had happened. Ethel sat, her eyes blank, her lips set, seeing, not the cheerful tea-table before her, but that hat, that grey material . . .

"You don't look too good yourself, my dear," said Miss Slater. "I hope you aren't starting 'flu."

"No, no," said Ethel wildly. "I'd almost welcome 'flu instead of —this!"

"Oh, my dear!" said Miss Slater, adding, with a sigh, "how strange everyone is to-day!"

"I'm sorry," said Ethel. "I'll just go in again now, shall I, and make sure that she's all right."

"Thank you, dear," said Miss Slater. "I'd be glad if you would. The whole thing seems to have got a bit beyond me somehow."

William, meanwhile, had not been wasting time. The gardener was returning to the greenhouse, the Outlaws were coming out of their hiding places, the coast was clear . . . Esmeralda must be removed from the scene of danger as quickly as possible. He came out from behind the sofa, removed the rug, placed Esmeralda on her feet, then—dived again into his hiding-place. He had heard footsteps approaching.

The door opened, and Ethel entered again. Esmeralda stood with her back to the door, the fall of veiling which trimmed the hat hiding her neck. The light was dim, but what Ethel could see was enough for her. Not only the hat, not only the material, but the very pattern of the dress was the one that Ethel had chosen herself. By some ghastly freak of chance, Mrs. Lane's mind and hers had had a single thought for their spring outfits. She gave a strangled cry and fled from the room.

Then William set to work. Ready hands assisted him, and soon Esmeralda was conveyed safely out of the drawing-room . . . out of the conservatory . . . into the darkening drive. So swift was the progress, so eager the helping hands that a whole row of potted freesias was swept off a shelf.

"Never mind!" said William. "We can't stay to pick them up . . . Where's the truck?"

"He took it," said Henry. "The gardener did. He found it there an' took it away, mutterin' to himself like mad. An' the sheet was in it too."

"It's jus' one horn of a dilemma after another," said Ginger.

"I told you it would get us into a muddle," said Douglas with gloomy satisfaction.

"Well, it hasn't done," said William spiritedly. "The ghost part didn't come off but that's all. Ethel didn't recognise Esmeralda or she'd have grabbed hold of it. An' it's goin' to be quite easy gettin' it back. We'll walk it."

"Walk it?" said Henry.

"Yes. It'll look jus' like a real person if we walk it. Ginger and me'll be on one side an' you two on the other an' we'll hold it up an' walk it along. It'll look as if we were goin' for a walk with a woman. No one'll know any diff'rent, an' I bet, even if Ethel's goin' home, we get there before her."

But Ethel was home first. She met Jimmy Moore at the gate and, letting down the defences of her pride, poured out her troubles to him in a flood of incoherent words. So incoherent were they, indeed, that at first Jimmy couldn't make head or tail of what she was saying. But that didn't matter. He was on his way to see her in order to bury the hatchet, and the hatchet seemed miraculously to have buried itself.

"WAIT TILL I GET HOLD OF THE LITTLE WRETCHES,"
SAID ETHEL.

"Oh, Jimmy," she moaned brokenly, "it's the most awful thing that's ever happened to me in my life and she's come out in them first so I shall never dare to wear them and I've spent *pounds* and *hours* on them. She must have written to the same shop for the same hat and gone to the same shop for the same material and got the same pattern out of the same book and I shall have to go on wearing that ghastly blue thing I wore all last spring, and I simply don't know how to go on living."

"Darling, what does it matter?" said Jimmy, with a vague—a very vague—idea what it was all about. "You look lovely in anything."

"Don't be silly," said Ethel. "You know I don't. But, Jimmy——"

"Yes?"

"I feel it's a sort of judgment on me for being so beastly to you about it. I feel that, if I'd gone to the pictures with you when you asked me, instead of wanting to run up the seams, this wouldn't have happened. I'm sorry, Jimmy."

"Oh, darling!"

The scene was set for a tender reconciliation, but, instead of yielding to the arm that Jimmy was tentatively slipping round her waist, Ethel stiffened suddenly, staring at the greenhouse, her eyes wide with horror.

"It's gone," she gasped. "My dress . . . It's been stolen. Oh, I was crazy to leave it there!"

But Jimmy's eyes had wandered from the greenhouse to a more arresting spectacle.

"What on earth's that?" he said, gazing open-mouthed at a strange group that had just appeared. Esmeralda was making her erratic progress down the road, swaying drunkenly from side to side, steered and supported in uncertain fashion by two boys on either side of her. There was a silence as Ethel slowly took in the identity of Esmeralda's supporters.

"Wait till I get hold of the little wretches," she said between her teeth.

She advanced down the road to meet the procession. The procession stopped. Ethel was only the vanguard. Behind her came the foreman of the decorators, who had returned to find that someone had been making hay of his cement and had a shrewd idea who the some-one was. Behind him came Mr. Brown, who had just discovered his distempered chest-of-drawers.

"Gosh!" said William, instinctively turning to retreat. But retreat was impossible. Two more figures were approaching from the opposite direction. The first was Mrs. Warwick's gardener, who had dis-covered the wreckage of his conservatory and had had little difficulty in tracing the culprits. Behind him came Miss Slater, fresh from a telephone conversation with Mrs. Lane, who had had no doubt at all of the identity of the pseudo-Hubert.

"Gosh!" repeated William. "Five! Five of 'em! I don't think anyone's ever got in five sep'rate rows at the same time before since the world began."

And then, with a certain sombre pride at his heart, still steering Esmeralda's drunken progress as best he could, he advanced to meet his fate. . . .